The Usual Story

Also by Libby Sommer and published by Ginninderra Press
My Year With Sammy
The Crystal Ballroom

Libby Sommer

The Usual Story

Versions of several chapters in this book were first
published as short stories in *Quadrant* magazine titled
'Tango', 'Painstaking Progress' and 'Tom'.

The characters and events in this book are fictitious, and any
resemblance to real persons, living or dead, is purely coincidental.

The Usual Story
ISBN 978 1 74027 579 2
Copyright © Libby Sommer 2018
Cover photo © A Little Buenos Aires

First published 2018 by
GINNINDERRA PRESS
PO Box 3461 Port Adelaide 5015
www.ginninderrapress.com.au

Contents

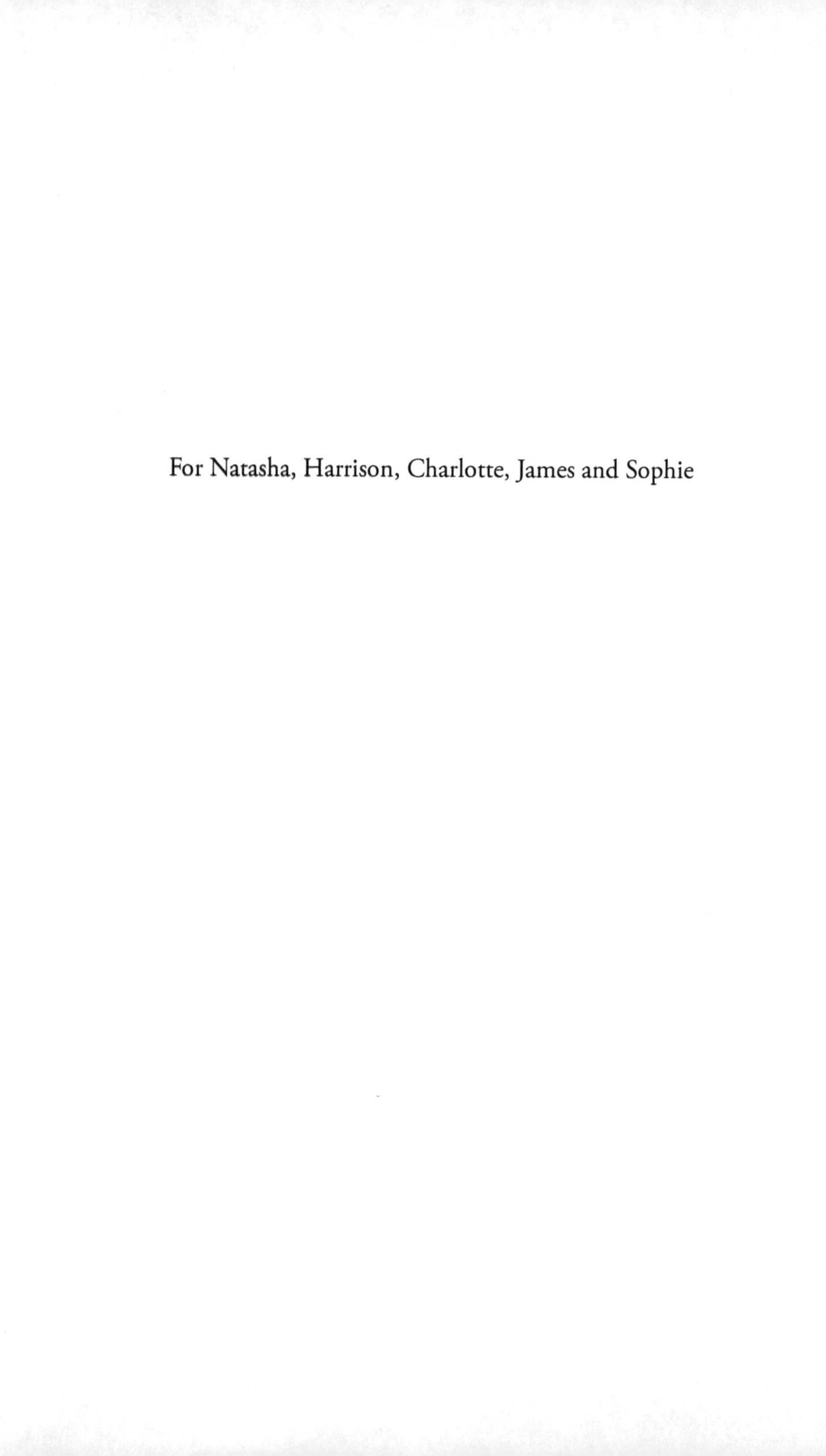
For Natasha, Harrison, Charlotte, James and Sophie

Part One

1

Tango

Tango is a passionate dance. A conversation between two people in which they can express every musical mood through steps and improvised movement.

Just before nine o'clock in the evening, I get out of my car and look up at the sky. I have sensed a shift in the weather. There is another breath of wind, a whispering in the air, but the clouds are stagnant against the dark night. I turn and move downhill towards the club, ejecting the chewing gum out of my mouth with a loud splat into the bushes, feel the first drops of rain on my bare arms. I pass the public phone box where frangipanis lie on the grass, pick one up, sniff at it, throw it back, then quickly enter the club.

It is not one of my best days. I don't know why. My dress is not uncomfortable, my skirt just right around the waist, the outfit not faded or balled, the black strappy shoes high, not too high, wrapped around my feet following the shape of my instep, and the new shampoo and conditioner make my hair curl naturally around my face. For reassurance, I stroke the pearl and bronze necklace nestled into the groove of my neck.

At reception, I pause to flash my card and take the lift to the third floor and then continue along the long hall, at the end of which is the thud and bounce of Latin American dance music.

I turn into the room, which is set up with tables and chairs in a horseshoe shape around the wooden dance floor, the DJ on the stage above and a bar at the back of the room. I see Nino down the front sitting with that older couple he usually sits with and wonder whether to join them or not. It is not easy coming to these places. It takes a whole day of psyching myself up.

'Sofia, you'll never find a rich husband if you're fat,' Mother had said, raising her glass. It was Mother's fifty-third birthday. Her hair was silvery with flecks of white now that she'd let her own natural colour grow through.

'How would you know?' Mother's youngest son, my brother, said, picking his nose and flicking the snot across the table at his mother.

Everyone said he was a radical, that boy. He did things a certain way. But somehow they still thought the sun shone out of his arse. Everyone laughed. The entire family – even Aunt Gertrude and Uncle Max and the two boy cousins – drinking the kosher wine at the Seder table. The moment passed.

Alone in my room, I sang along with the radio station, turned way up. 'The Happy Wanderer'. 'I love to go a wandering along the mountain streams, and as I go I love to sing, my knapsack on my back.'

I would practise my leaps across the room in front of the mirror. See how far I could cross in one amazing jump, my back leg extended behind me as I leapt into the air from a running start.

Usually Nino has a few dances with me at the Friday night dance at Randwick. Now that he is semi-retired, he dances four nights a week, plays tennis and works out at the gym when he's not working part-time as an accountant. He has grey hair combed back from a high forehead and around his neck is a brown leather thong with a small silver medallion. The leather thong makes him look more attractive, more unusual, more interesting. He likes to show the younger women how to dance.

The tall Portuguese man with the dyed black hair (I assume it's dyed), described Nino as a vampire. But then he is probably jealous of the number of different women that Nino is able to get to join him at his table.

Jordan, the taxi driver, who dances to keep his weight down, said that Nino only likes to dance the tango so he can feel the women's breasts pressed against him.

'He didn't say that,' I said in disbelief. 'Nino is a gentleman, he wouldn't say that.'

Jordan was ready to wave Nino over to confirm the story.

Sometimes I sit by myself with my coat on the chair beside me, pretending I am here with a friend, and the friend is on the dance floor and that's why I am sitting alone.

I work freelance and I'm working on a book of family history that I have been commissioned to write. Things have changed very much, several times, since I grew up, and like everyone in Sydney, I have led several lives and I still lead some of them. Since I started the book, I have gone out with two South American tango dancers, one Irish dance teacher, and a revolutionary playwright who patted my thigh and said, 'Where is this relationship going? I would like it to be more. My wife isn't interested in sex any more.'

My children are grown up and lead their own lives. Sometimes the randomness, the sheer unpredictability of the way I am living, what I am doing, fills me with delight.

For six months, I have been seeing a man from Leichhardt. As far as I can see, this is over. I call him J, as if he were a character in a novel that pretends to be true.

J is the first letter of his name, but I chose it also because it seems to suit him. The letter J seems to give a promise of youth and vitality. It is upright and strong, with very straight vertebrae. And using just the letter, not needing a name, is in line with a system I often employ these days. I say to myself, France, 1993, and I see a whole succession of scenes, the apricots and salmons of the buildings and the turquoise of the Mediterranean Sea.

'Dressed for salsa?' said Dr Ross with a grin as he closed the door behind me.

'I don't remember telling you that I danced salsa,' I said as he extracted my file from the drawer of the metal filing cabinet. 'I think you're getting me confused with someone else.'

'In O'Connell Street or Liverpool Street. I can picture it.'

'I used to dance at Glebe Town Hall on Sunday nights, but that was ages ago.'

'Your salsa phase,' he confirmed. He moved from the filing cabinet to the large grey seat opposite me. 'Any stallions beating at your door?' he said with a note of expectancy in his voice.

'They're all pathetic. It's hopeless.'

He gasped in a pretending way.

'Not all of them,' I corrected myself. 'Just the ones I engage with.'

He wrote that down.

'It's all over with the fireman,' I volunteered. 'He's married anyway.'

'You can cross fireman off the list now.'

'I've been through the list. It's been so many years. I've met one of everything.'

'Z,' he said with a smirk. 'Of course. Zookeeper.'

I shrugged, remembering the organic gardener. 'I've probably met one of those too.'

The last time I saw J, or rather, what I thought would be the last time I saw J, I was standing at the turnstiles at Town Hall station and he came through the gate sweating, his face and body flushed, his hair damp.

It was a hot night in September. We'd had a meal together at a Spanish restaurant in the city. I remember how flushed his skin was, but have to imagine his boots, his broad white thighs as he crouched or sat, and the open friendly expression he must have worn on his face, talking to me, the person who wanted nothing from him any more. I know I was conscious of how I looked standing there under the neon light, and that in this glare I might seem even older to him than I was, and also that he might find me less attractive.

He went to get a cup of coffee, then came back out. He stood beside me and looked down with his arm almost around me. I sensed his hesitation about touching me. I kissed him on the cheek and he looked deep into my eyes and I knew what he wanted me to say. Saw the pleading expression he must have worn on his face.

'Have you lost weight?' I ask Dan, one of my regular dance partners, as I flick my foot back and behind his knee into a *gancho*. The movement is like a horse trying to shake its shoe from its hoof.

'Make sure your heel is up when you do the *gancho*,' Alfred had told me. 'Sweep your leg along the floor and out. Not up with the leg, but up with the heel.'

I remind myself to make sure my shoulders are down. Firm arms, shoulders down. I'm sure that's why I get so much neck pain; my shoulders must be up around my ears.

Alfred, bald, shiny-headed Alfred, who Nino says looks like a gangster with his shaved head and black T-shirt, still thinks everyone on the dance floor sets out to block his movement around the room. There's no doubt about him. At least he started out friendly enough.

Dan smells good for a change and he's lost his big stomach that used to come between us. Sometimes I would gag with the smell of him.

'Yes,' he says as we bounce lightly to the beat of a *milonga*. 'I got sick with the flu for a couple of weeks last year and decided to keep the weight off.'

During a break in the sets, I sit down next to Alfred.

'What do I look like?' Alfred says, inclining his head towards the dance floor. 'I wish I knew what I looked like.'

'I don't know,' I say. 'I wasn't watching you.'

He sighs with disappointment.

And he's made up a step. I must tell him I don't want to do his stupid made-up step, which is a cross with my left leg, but when I feel his opposite hip against mine I don't know if it's a *gancho* or not. The main problem, which I must tell him, is that he pulls me off my axis, my centre.

'Would you do it if it wasn't made-up?' he says now we're up and dancing a *vals*.

'It's not that I won't do it,' I say. 'I can't do it. I'm not deliberately not doing it,' I say, unable to disguise my anger. Should I make a scene and leave the dance floor and leave him standing there because he's being so rude and aggressive because I can't do his stupid made-up step?

'Do you speak to the other women like you speak to me?' I say, not caring who can hear.

'I can't understand why you won't do it.'

'I *can't* do it.'

'I wish I knew what that little voice was saying in your head.'

His hip pushes hard into me, very hard, so I am forced into a backward lock from the left leg.

Wheep wheep, wheep wheep, wheep wheep went the big shiny knife against the hard grey stone. Father would carve the roast lamb each week for the Sunday lunch. After lunch we'd go to the hospital to visit Grandpa. Grandpa without his left leg, then without his right leg. Gangrene. He died piece by piece. Left foot, left leg. Right foot, right leg.

When Father came back from the factory in the evenings, my brother and I, pale and silent, would join him for his dinner. After dinner, Father listened to the radio in the lounge with his newspaper, and at seven Mother, having washed up, joined him. The family were together only at dinner, after which Mother and Father sat behind their newspapers and the children went upstairs to their rooms. Sometimes a stupid child would pull the wings off a fly or even a butterfly and watch it suffer.

When I was nine, Mother said, 'You're an introvert. I was like you when I was your age. I hardly said a word to anyone.' She brought her teeth together and closed her lips in a line in that all-knowing way of hers. Through the Passover songs, the questions, the answers, the accusation, the spoken prayers, she sat silent on the chair beside me, all self-contained. She swallowed the Jewish religion just like she did as a Catholic. She sang along with its tales of prosecution and banishment and arrival at the Land of Israel.

She closed her mouth, so I said, 'What's an introvert?'

'The opposite of extrovert,' she said. 'Your Uncle Max is an extrovert.'

I looked over to his flushed face and his bulbous nose and the sound of his voice joining in the songs. Everyone in their Sunday best and me in my school uniform.

'Sing,' she scolded. 'I can't see your mouth moving.'

'I'll fill in a form for you to have a blood test whenever you want,' said the GP. 'You won't have to come and see me first. You can go straight there.' He walked over to his desk. 'Anything else you want tested?'

'You'd better add iron. And the test for blood sugar. A family history of diabetes.'

At the pathologist across the road, the nurse tightened the strap around my arm. 'Those arms look like they've done a lot of work,' she said.

'What do you mean? How can you tell?'

'The veins. You've got good veins. The veins are connected to the muscles.'

The women at the dances look beautiful in a cruel way, with their blood-red lips and their nails long and sharp. They're not very friendly. I am just a casual, after all. I haven't signed up for a ten-week course and I don't go to the beginners' lesson at seven-thirty.

Things have not changed very much on the dance scene since I started there so many years ago. 'Same old, same old,' as I heard the Turkish woman describe the previous Saturday's dance at Marrickville to the Egyptian woman with the red red lips.

'What a beautiful smile you have,' said the woman on the door who takes the money. 'Did anyone tell you that your whole face smiles when you smile?'

She's nice. She's the partner of the man who runs the dance. She says she doesn't mind that she doesn't get to dance on the Friday nights because she dances nearly every other night of the week at the lessons. She's very beautiful. Russian with long blonde hair against her tanned smooth olive skin, very long shiny legs and always one of her very short cut-up-the-side skirts that she makes herself. She's my age.

A new man makes his way around the dance floor. Good posture. Straight back, strong arm position. Looks like he'd be a good strong lead.

The music stops and he comes over and sits on the spare seat beside me.

'It's all too heat-making for an old man like me,' he jokes as he fans himself furiously with a Bingo brochure. 'I'm a postman from Perth on holiday in Sydney,' he says by way of an introduction in a well-modulated English voice. 'I could have had a two-week holiday in Paris for the price of his three-day trip to Sydney.'

I smile. 'Have you read *The Post Office* by Charles Bukowski?'

'We're not very cultural in Perth.'

'You speak very well for a postman.'

'Well,' he shrugs, as if that is a whole other story that he will not go into at this stage. 'Dancing the tango allows me to meet famous people all over the world,' he says. 'In Paris, London, New York. My name is Fabian, by the way.'

'That's a very romantic name. I grew up in the era of Fabian the pop star.'

'In Perth, we all live in one big Waiting Room,' he adds. 'We're all waiting. Not much culture or adventure. There are many French and Italian-speaking women who dress like the women you see in Paris. The tango community is very close. If one person learns a new step, then everyone learns it. Two weeks later, we're all doing it.'

'You've lost weight,' Dr Ross said when I first walked in.

I shrugged. 'It's wonderful what black does. Just one item of black.'

He looked down at his shoes with the regular pattern of holes punched towards the pointed toes. 'What about black shoes?' he asked.

'Your feet look smaller,' I reassured him.

'You know what they say about small feet.' He laughed.

I assumed he meant small feet, small penis. I sat down opposite him, a box of tissues between us on the small square table. 'It's hands,' I said. 'Not feet. Fingers.'

He uncapped his pen, looked down at his notes.

'You're not going to start on that track already, are you?' I said. 'Not so early in the session.'

'I grew up dancing the polka in Italy,' says Nino as we turn into a Viennese waltz.

'How was your holiday?' I ask.

'Very boring.'

'Didn't you play tennis with your grandsons?'

He pulls a face. 'Did you meet any nice European men while you were away?' he says.

'I was married to an Austrian. From Vienna.'

'Did you see him there?'

'He lives in Sydney.' I say this simply to establish that I had a husband once, that I have been married, and to a European man, an interesting man, a man of cultural heritage. I want to assure Nino that I was not always alone, unattached.

'Does Anthony ask you to dance?' Nino asks.

'No, he doesn't.'

'He should.'

'There are no shoulds. I asked him once and he went off across the floor doing his own thing. It was very humiliating.'

Nino nods and grins with no understanding in his demeanour.

'Anthony has many choices,' he says, as if that would explain it. 'He's young and he's a good dancer. A lot of the women are after him.

I remember Mother saying to me when I was a teenager, 'It's a man's world.' But Mother had two children by the time she was seventeen.

My own daughter, Kate, is an artist. Sometimes I mind her two children while Kate goes out painting. This afternoon I was over at her house looking after the baby and the two-year-old.

'I feel like Superman when I mind the kids and then go out tango dancing,' I like to tell my friends. 'At three o'clock I'm on the oval kicking a football around with my grandson and then at seven-thirty I'm changing into my tight skirt with a split up the side and my red top and my strappy high-heeled shoes and I'm out the door again. Like Clarke Kent changing into his Superman cape.'

'Have you got a dance partner?' my friends, or maybe my brother, might ask.

'Various,' I would say. 'I've got various. Several.'

Today when Kate got back, I told her I had brought the washing in because it had started to sprinkle with rain.

'Was it dry?'

'I think so.'

'You think so?'

'Well, I was rushing to bring it in before it poured with rain and I had two children to look after at the same time and the baby was awake and the noise of the builders next door and the electrician with his ladder and his cords everywhere and I couldn't even get to the toilet.'

'Well, when you brought the washing in, did you do all the ironing? Did you iron all the clothes when you brought them in?'

We both laughed. It was a joke.

'I think the baby looks like me,' I said to my daughter one day when she reached for the old brown photo album.

'Have a look,' I said pointing to a photograph of myself in Class 8. 'Here I am. Can you see me?'

'Oh, yes.'

'I'm the one on the end. The little Miss Perfect sitting up so straight.'

'You do look different to the others.'

'I'm the one trying too hard.'

'You're the only one wearing a tie.'

I don't really own a tight skirt with a split up the side, but I wish I did have one. And nice long legs to show off. Instead, I usually wear the same pair of black trousers that I hope will slim me down, and one of my many pretty tops. Well, actually, that's not true either. I wear the same black camisole top, or one of the two similar black camisole tops, and a sheer cardigan on the top to disguise, to cover, to conceal, to pretend, that my arms aren't so fat, that my freckled skin doesn't look so blotchy in the light. But usually it gets so hot I have to strip down to the black pants and the black camisole top with my hair pulled high on top of my head so it doesn't hang in wet cats' tails around my face.

'Can we get a photocopy of her?' Alfred says as Jordan comes over and leads me towards the dance floor.

Jordan's style is firm and masculine. I like the smell of the mint that he always sucks or chews. After a good half hour of dancing in the hot auditorium, he speaks. 'If they have a Latin bracket,' he says, 'will you dance it with me?'

Afterwards, we sit back at Nino's table with the much older couple.

'You and Jordan dance well together,' says the man so stiff with arthritis it takes him a long time to stand up, to unwrap his legs and put his whole weight on his feet. But he does. He gets up each week to dance with his lady friend and they shuffle around over in a dark corner after a couple of glasses of white wine and when they are into their second packet of potato chips.

'You look like you should be married,' the older man continues. 'Like you should have babies together.'

'Who? Me and Jordan?' I say, trying to sound casual about the possibility of me and Jordan. I quite like him. But only because he dances salsa and rumba and rock and roll so well. He smells nice, he dances well, what more could I wish for? But of course Jordan has a regular girlfriend; the girlfriend doesn't come to the Friday night dances.

Jordan laughs. 'She's a grandmother already,' he says with a dismissive flick of his hand towards me. 'We couldn't have children together.'

'Here's a photo of Grandpa and me. I'm standing beside Grandpa's wheelchair. It's a black and white picture that shows him only from just above the knees, which is where the rug would have ended that covers his lap. I look about thirteen in this picture. My tall gawky stage. Long hair pulled back severely, a cardigan to hide my developing breasts. Mother hated my hair. I think she must have spent her whole life telling me how dreadful my hair looked. I'm smiling in the photo and leaning down to put my face a little bit closer to Grandpa.'

I was eleven when my brother told me that my much older brother and sister were not my real brother and sister. I cried so much he had to send for someone to find Mother and Father.

My half-brother still hates Mother, to this day.

'I feel sorry for him,' I said to my half-sister, Inez. 'That at his age he's still obsessing about all that stuff.'

'Lots of people have had difficult childhoods,' Inez snapped. 'His childhood was no worse than plenty of others.' Then she added, 'I'm so sick of hearing about him and Mother.'

My half-sister used to read stories to me when I was a child. I can't remember at what age Inez left home to get married and stopped reading to me. I must have been four. Perhaps I was older. Mother was always far too busy to read stories. When Mother was a girl, a woman's place was in the home. Someone neglected to tell Mother. If they had, she would simply have told them she needed to help Father in the business or they'd go bankrupt again.

A bird chimes in a cheerful tone and the leaves of the jacaranda tree whisper in the wind. The beautiful jacaranda tree. We had one like that once. I thought I'd miss that tree and that house but although I did at first, after a while I came to love the different place I moved to. And then this place where I live now, by the sea, the place where J came to live with me. The place where we pretended we could live together. Where he went off to work every day and I kissed him goodbye at the front door. The place where he'd come home to me at night.

'Step further across for the forward *ochos*,' said the visiting Argentinian dance teacher. 'Step further back behind me for the turn and swivel. Keep your left hip down when doing a forward *ocho*. Caress the floor with your feet. No feet in the air. Relax your right shoulder. Keep your shoulders down. Do the cross whether the man leads you into it or not.' (I think that's what he said.) 'Be heavy on the front foot in the cross. Weight forward. Keep your knees together when you do an adornment. Keep the adornments simple. Just do one or two. Polish the leg and then down again; then step over. Slow down on the turns. Don't run. Keep your right wrist firm. In the open embrace, let your arms go up and down the man's arm. Up to behind his neck and then down to his forearm.'

'You've had a lesson with the best,' said Pedro.

'I've been saving myself,' I'd answered proudly.

I'm remembering a Friday. It must have been about six-thirty. Early summer. The bougainvilleas and the jacarandas were already in bloom but no frangipanis yet. I'd been waiting for J to come home, looking forward to his return from the city, hoping we'd sit together with a drink outside on the balcony. He'd have a shower and get changed and then we'd go out for the meal that he'd promised me.

Instead, he was on the phone, his face slightly in shadow but well lit enough for me to see the ever-present cigarette. Half inside, half outside so he could exhale out the door. His voice droned on and on. The wind increased in force. A strong wind, blowing against my head, my hair, my hands. My furious heart beat hard against the walls of my ribs. Then the wind died down again and I could only hear his voice; not the sound of the birds any more or the movement of the leaves on the trees.

It rained a lot that night. The sound of the waterfall below. The sound of water after rain.

At dusk, the last of the brightness of the pink sighs above the horizon. The sea a woolly blanket of blue and white. The same four palm trees all in a row between the road and the beach. The pale face of the moon two thirds of the way to the sky. One-eighth of the side of its face missing but still the moon looks down, almost expressionless. A woman flashes the blue of her helmet as she cycles with strong thighs up Bronte Road, head bent in concentration on the road ahead as a bus bellows black dust. The pink of the sky turns into mauve mixed with blue as the French cook arrives with his pale blue scarf knotted like a boy scout's. It's tight around his neck. With his right hand he checks his balls for reassurance as he mounts the step into the café.

It's unusual for me to be outside these days, but no more odd than spending hours inside at the Mitchell Library looking at microfilm or walking through Waverley Cemetery looking for graves, no more odd than my work, or the people stuck on hot trains and buses trying to get home from work, or other places where people find themselves as they struggle to get through their days.

Times change, your life changes and you need to shift.

There were huge waves out to sea after the winds of the night before. The biggest waves I have ever seen, in fact. They really were magnificent. During the night, I listened to the winds as they thrashed the ocean waves through the branches of the trees.

'At our age, we're not going to improve our game of tennis,' the man on Bare Island said.

'Speak for yourself,' I said.

'It's all your fault anyway,' I said to Dr Ross.

He looked puzzled.

'You said to me, "It's your body. You can do what you like with it," in that moralising tone of yours.'

'I would have only said that,' he said gently, 'if I thought you were being too generous with your body.'

'After that bit of moralising, I've turned that whole side of myself off. Anyway, I have no libido. So it's not such an issue any more.'

'Well, that's good.' He took a sip of his coffee that surely must be cold already. 'There's more to me than you think,' he said.

'You're very blinkered,' I said. I held up my hands beside my face to imitate a horse with covers at the side of his eyes. 'Straight. You haven't got an open mind. In some areas,' I clarified.

He pulled a face.

'I bet your daughter, or daughters, tell you that.'

'They're too polite.'

'Your daughter looked lovely, by the way. The one I saw last time.'

'The blonde?'

'Yes. I thought you had a son and a daughter.'

'No. I've got three daughters.'

'Three daughters? And a son?'

'Yes. So you think I need to open my chakras?' he joked.

I shrugged. 'Chakras spin, they don't open.'

'You might be surprised. I could be a Buddhist.'

'Is my time up?' I said with an anxious glance at the clock.

'It's okay,' he reassured me. 'I hadn't noticed.'

Little by little, I'd learned new things about J. Once, when staying with him in that first summer, I found him lying on my bed with so pitiful a look on his face that I couldn't see into it. It was very painful to realise how utterly defeated he looked; everything about him was different to what I'd seen before, out of sync, closed down, remote, his very guts hanging out in front of me. He looked up at me from a place so removed it was as if I was a stranger. I lay down beside him and put my arms around him. He turned away, closed his eyes.

Only since then did I become fully aware of his illness. He was so totally exposed to me, the reality of his situation, and his condition was so distressing that at some moments it was as if I suffered it too, that I had become part of him and part of it.

I'm getting up later these days, that's the hardest time for me; I have to force myself to do things. Mere existence has become a struggle. Some days are just too hard to bear. Dr Ross said I should go out for a walk when I feel like this. So I spend whole days out, roaming around and do not return until it is dark.

I find I can really talk to Dr Ross. He's someone I can confide in. Thinking back, I'm surprised, in fact, about how much I've told him. It's when telling him things that I can really remember. This comforts me. And he knows what's wrong with me; he's given a name to my condition.

The brown bird with a black triangle on his head jumps on the green see-saw of a branch. Up and down he goes, up and down, until he flies off again in a southerly direction.

'The bastards,' Dr Ross said as a joke, with a tilt of his head and a puffing out of his cheeks as if he was about to spit on the ground in disgust.

'I love it when you do that,' I said. 'That's the way it is exactly.'

It's not true that talking about J has helped me. He has not stopped being my obsession. Talking about him has not, as I first imagined, been a remembering of a completed period of my life, but only a continuous charade at remembering, in the form of words. Even now, I sometimes wake up suddenly, as though he's still beside me, my heart heavy and thudding with the feeling that life is slipping away from me, minute by minute. The space around me in the darkness is so still that the things in my world retreat into nothingness. In another minute, they will disappear completely. Listening in the darkness to every creak, to every tiny sound, it's as if there's someone out there wanting to take my life. I keep the light on in the hallway, hoping to keep this fear of death at bay.

This need to talk about J, which I felt so strongly when he first left me, is gradually dying away and I fall back into a dreary wordlessness with which I am very familiar.

Back home after the dance, I go straight to my room. I turn on the lamp and kneel on the bed to pile the cushions up. Tears come almost to my eyes, my stomach is empty with sadness. It is all such a bloody fantasy. I stare around at the night silence, then huddle in my bed.

I had a box of a hundred Dilmah tea bags that I'd bought especially for J. When the box is empty, I'd told myself, the pain will have eased.

Months later, I walked outside to the balcony, sat on the chaise lounge that we'd chosen together and looked down the gully at the grey sea. I drank the last tea bag from the box.

The tea was strong and hot, and so bitter it parched my tongue.

2

Milonga

The word *milonga* means the music of a dance that preceded the tango. *Milonga* is quicker and more upbeat than tango, usually in 2/4 time. *Milonga* also means a dance, where people go to dance tango and *milonga*.

From the balcony, I can see my friend Victor as he eases his long legs out of the small Honda sedan and looks over at the Pacific Ocean that he said he could see all the way down the hill. He said he thought he knew where my street was, but has ended up coming the wrong way around the eastern seaboard. But at least he rang and said he'd be late.

He pauses at the foot of the stairs, breathes in the autumn crispness in the afternoon air even though the humidity is still high. There is a whisper of wind, a shooshing sound from the waves, and the tall palms sway. 'I'd like to add you to my list of people that I can meet for a coffee,' he'd said on the phone. 'I don't mind coming over your way. I'd like to explore a different part of Sydney. And I haven't seen your new kitchen yet.' His red T-shirt is worn loose over his beige cotton trousers so as not to stick to his stomach. His open sandals are strapped firmly at the ankles.

The block of units where I live sits astride an overgrown gully that leads to a beach. Recently I moved my desk from the study into the bedroom so that I can see the changing moods of the sea as I work.

'I've moved my desk into the bedroom,' I said to Victor.

'You've brought the mountain to Mohammed,' he joked. 'You

can just roll over in bed and say, hold it a moment while I write that thought down.'

In the mornings, I have to decide whether to leave the apartment from the back door and then re-enter from the front as if arriving at work or whether to just roll out of bed and sit on the cane chair in front of the desk.

There are whole days of solitary confinement, days in which my only activity is walking two or three steps from the bed to the desk. Sometimes I just sit here in my nightgown watching the horizon change colour as my own warm smell rises from the opening of my collar.

My childhood fantasy for my life in the future was to be confined alone inside a prison cell. The idea of being forced to live in a room by myself appealed to me because I would be allowed to read all the books that I wanted and to order all my favourite foods. I didn't desire or imagine myself to be in the company of other people; just a hand through a slot in the door that delivered the books and the food.

When J lived here, for a short time my work space was in the spare room, the room with a narrow window that looks out over the tops of palms, frangipani trees and a red hibiscus bush.

'If you let him move in, he'll pull you down with him,' a friend had warned, 'and you'll never dig him out.'

The window is sealed shut and soundproofed, but through the wall I can hear cars driving in towards their garages, doors closing, voices, the back door slamming, the splash of water as someone washes their car, or the music from a car radio.

I'd have the computer on and ready to go as I'd watch J have another cigarette or another cup of coffee while I waited for him to leave. My memory of this time remains clear, although there are variations in the parts I dwell on.

Victor turns and walks up the hill, climbs the steps, feels the salt-laden air on his freshly shaven face and presses the security button. He waits, then says, 'Dancing Queen? Is that the Dancing Queen?'

I laugh before buzzing him in and then, with a nervous flick of hair, open the door of the unit to await his arrival down the steps. I look away as he appears at the top, not wanting to watch any awkwardness or self-consciousness that may be apparent as he makes his way down. I've dressed carefully, in the end deciding on a high-necked cotton top and trousers, making sure not to give any wrong impressions. We've known each other a long time, since childhood, but this is the first time we are meeting up since his separation from his wife.

At the tango lesson this week, the dance teacher told us we have to keep our emotions inside us when we dance. We were practising dancing between chairs, with a partner, one leading, one following, eyes closed.

'You don't have to keep your enjoyment of the music and the dancing inside you,' he'd said, surveying his students in the church hall. 'But you mustn't get upset when you bump into someone, or when someone treads on your toe or when a woman's stiletto heel spears you in the foot.'

'So where's the kitchen then?' Victor asks after kissing me hello, one cheek and then the other. He walks in front of me down the hallway. At the doorway to the galley-style kitchen he stops and says, 'Wow.'

I can't see his face. Does he mean it? Is he really impressed by what I've done with the kitchen? That's what we talked about the first time on the phone when I rang to see which real estate agent he was using, now that I was thinking of moving, and now that Victor's ex-wife was pushing for the sale of their family home. We talked about the 'wow factor' that the real estate agents refer to.

I step in front of him into the kitchen and show him the pull-out pantry, the integrated dishwater, the silestone bench top, point to the red glass splashback.

'I wondered when you'd get to that bit,' he says with reverence in his tone. 'Bold. You made a bold choice.'

After it ended with J, I made a conscious decision to add more red to my life. A touch of red in every room: in the cushions, the paintings, the ceramic plates on the walls, the burgundy bedspread.

I walk in front of Victor along the hallway as the sun streams in on to the pale aqua carpet and the soft apricot walls. 'I'll show you the rest of the place.' I nod in the direction of the main bedroom. 'I may as well show you in here.'

As soon as he enters the room, he asks about the desk by the window. 'Your work is always in front of you,' he says.

'Seven days and nights a week.'

'Where's the TV, though?'

'I was thinking about a TV in here,' I gesture, 'putting it up on the wall on a pivotelli.'

'You can get in practice for when you're lying in a hospital bed,' Victor says. He rubs his chin with the back of his hand. He looks so much like his sister, my friend from school days: coarse thick hair, dark arched eyebrows, curved nose, solid features. Polish heritage.

'I thought you might have a good idea about where I could put a television set,' I say. 'You're the expert on all the latest equipment.'

He smiles knowingly, looks up at the headless nude on the wall painted by my daughter and says, 'With the new flat screens, you could replace that painting with a monitor. They even put paintings inside the screens so you wouldn't know it was a TV.'

I frown. 'I won't be doing that. I could have a television here on this little table but you wouldn't be able to see it from both sides of the bed because the foot of the bed is so high.'

'You're right,' he says. 'If there's a second person in the bed, they won't be able to see over the top. Maybe your pivotelli idea is the best.'

'It would be nice to lie in bed watching TV on a cold winter's night.' I sigh.

Through the tiny dust-encrusted wire bars of the fly-screen are the terracotta-tiled roofs, television aerials attached to the chimneys, balancing up there near the sky as the clouds thicken over towards the west.

'I lie in bed watching TV on a summer's night,' he laughs, expecting me to join in the joke because it's summer and he's spending his evenings in bed watching television.

'Really?' I say with a frown, perceiving the point he is making.

The door bangs open as we step out on to the balcony. The afternoon sun has moved over to the other side of the building, the balcony in shadow. We look out to sea as the waves roll in and break again in big white fans of froth. The waves crash, then jump with a rumble and a whoosh. The real estate agent said I have a half beach view but actually you can see only a small corner of the beach if you stand all the way to the left.

'I suppose you eat breakfast out here,' Victor says.

I don't say, no, I don't, that I have to keep out of the sun. Instead, I walk over to the corner where you can see more of the sea. 'You can see the beach from here.'

Victor has to squash between the round glass table and the sliding door to get to the corner of the balcony. I hope there won't be a problem with him being too big to fit between the table and the glass. I could move the table, but I want him to be able to fit through.

We stand for a long time at the railing looking out at the trees in the gully. Out to sea, a line of turquoise darkens before transforming into a wave. The wave crashes, widens, merges. The next wave follows and then it too disappears into white.

I'd fallen in love only once before. My husband may have come to love me in return, but I don't know that. 'I married you because you were suitable,' he'd said. 'I wasn't wearing rose-coloured glasses.'

Yesterday, the bamboo in the gully was lit by the early morning sun, the palms and ferns dark, camouflaged in the shadows. The sun glowed gold over to the left. The sun was there behind the glass and steel of the new apartment block. I looked up at the heavily overcast sky and reminded myself that the sun hadn't disappeared. It was still there, but hidden. On the radio a voice said, 'The wild flowers are expected to come alive after the rain.'

I think that when you are really stuck, when you have stood still in the same place for far too long, it's almost as if a bomb needs to go off, to get you to move, to get you to jump, and then to hope for the best. It has to occur as a desperate act to get some momentum happening.

Victor leans closer when he points to a tree or a building and his arm almost touches my shoulder.

On the ocean, a board rider skates across its surface before he too is buried in an instant beneath the thunderous swell.

'Don't jump in,' Dr Ross had said. 'Stay on the edge of the pool.'

We climb the stairs into the afternoon brightness and begin walking to the strip of cafés by the beach. At the top of the hill that leads to Bronte Park, we look down at the children's playground with its sandpit and the roundabout and the two slippery dips – one small, one large. Victor loosens the Velcro strips of his sandals as we admire the park and the beach below. The cubby house in the middle of the sandpit is all wrapped up with masking tape. When on earth are the council going to get round to fixing the equipment?

'This is where I bring my grandchildren to play,' I say.

'Do you see much of them?'

'Once or twice a week I help out. I've volunteered to do that. I want to have a close relationship with them.'

'You enjoy it, though, don't you?'

'Yes. But it nearly kills me. It exhausts me totally. Physically and emotionally.'

'You can come home and watch television in bed,' he says.

'I come home, lie on the bed, and stare at the ceiling.'

Last night, willy wagtails twittered in the trees and a soft breeze from the north rustled the backlit green of the leaves. I breathed in the cool air – the sweet, slightly exotic scent of spring – then looked up at the deep unknowable night; three stars visible between the low hanging cloud and the darkened sky, the clouds full and bunched and draped with grey. Higher up, the clouds expanded and thickened then disappeared into black. And there was the ghost moon hanging to the east, enormous and simple in its circular arcs.

I rang Aunt Gertrude at the Montefiore Home to see how things were going with her and Uncle Max. Uncle Max was Father's brother.

'It's so sad,' she said. 'He's back from the hospital. He came back on Friday. It's very sad. He can't talk and he can't walk and he can't feed himself.'

'It must have been very traumatic for him having that operation.'

'No, it's not that. This is his type of dementia. When I put the TV on he has a look, though. Sometimes when he's asleep, I wish he would just slip away. The doctor asked me if I want him resurrected if he has a heart attack or a stroke. I said no. "Do you mind if I document that?" said the doctor. He's got a nice room. When he looks up, he can see to the river. Yesterday, I noticed he took the juice from the nurse and fed himself. He doesn't converse at all. That infection has gone right to the bone. He's in good hands. It's a wonderful hospital. I was thinking about your dad just the other day,' she added after a pause.

'How come?'

'Because it was his birthday and the day he died.'

'That' s right. Aren't I dreadful for not remembering?'

'No.'

Victor and I head down the hill and across the park to Bronte Road. We cross the street and find a seat in a café that overlooks the water.

A waiter comes to take our order.

'It looks deserted here today,' I say.

The waiter's long brown hair hangs loose on his shoulders, all bright and shiny near his forehead. He looks up and down the street outside. 'Looks like a bomb's gone off.'

'Maybe because it's suddenly turned cold this afternoon.'

He pulls out a notepad from the pocket of his apron, opens it up. 'Bronte's funny like that. It goes in waves.'

A parking policeman in a wide-brimmed grey felt hat paces it out up the footpath on the other side of the road. A woman runs out of the café and across the road and gets to her car just in time.

We order coffees and talk about the course in personal growth that Victor is attending.

'I stood up and said, I've made a choice to live a single life now,' he says with pride.

'You've made many choices over the years,' I remind him. 'With Marilyn. It didn't happen overnight.'

'That's right.'

'It was your choice all the way along the line.'

He nods.

'She said a long time ago she was going to leave when the girls turned eighteen, didn't she?'

He sits up straighter in the chair. 'Not exactly. Not in those words. But what about you? You've been through all this.'

Out on the ocean, three wetsuited surfers paddle gently away from the shore, the ocean still and quiet but always moving. A wave builds up, a surfer just ahead of its tumbling white mane.

'I married as a teenager.'

'Marilyn wasn't much older.'

'I married a man I'd been brought up to marry. Successful. Jewish. I only knew him six months. He swept me off my feet.'

'We knew each other six weeks. Six weeks and we were married.'

Overhead comes the roar of a plane as it curves towards the north. The plane is all white shiny metal against pale blue sky.

'I thought six months was quick.'

'We didn't really know each other. But it was hot,' he says proudly.

'Why do you think your sister never married?'

'Shyness. We're both shy.'

He seems smaller sitting there when he says this. The small uncertain boy. I'm surprised to see it.

He gives me a look that expects me to understand, to show compassion, to show tenderness even. As far as I can see, I've lost my compassion. I lost it a while ago now. After J left, it was the misery of knowing that I'd done it to myself again, been drawn in by my own stupid need to rescue lame ducks. You idiot, I think, still furious. You stupid fool.

We leave the café and walk out into the afternoon shadows heading back to my house. At Cross Street, where we climb the final flight of stairs, I feel Victor looking at me from behind as he follows me up

'These are the last steps,' I reassure him.

'You're probably fitter than me.'

'Well, I'm at the gym five times a week. And two nights dancing. That's seven times a week.'

He shakes his head. 'I'm exhausted just hearing all the things you do. The only exercise I get is opening and closing my hand.'

I sigh. 'People always react that way. So I usually don't say.'

At the front door, we stop.

'I won't ask you in,' I say, concerned that I should have said something earlier in order to avoid this potential awkwardness at the door. 'You probably don't want to come in anyway,' I add, trying to imply that it isn't my choice that he's not coming in. 'I'm going out to a dance lesson tonight.'

'What time do you go?'

'Seven-thirty,' I lie, unable to make an open declaration about needing time to myself before going out. 'I often don't feel like going. But it's good for me. I've got a little community now because I go regularly.'

'That's what they tell us at this course I'm doing. Set up communities.'

We kiss goodbye, once on the cheek, and then he leans down and offers his other cheek.

'Your shout next time,' he calls out as he walks to his car.

In late March, I'd visited Aunt Gertrude at the Montefiore Home and asked her for memories of Father.

'Your father!' she'd said. 'I can't tell you that. But I can tell you about your grandparents. What I know. You ask the questions and I'll try and give the answers.'

We were sitting at a round table in the cafeteria eating smoked salmon sandwiches and drinking tea when she said something that shocked me. She'd looked into her empty cup and then looked up at me. I started to stand up, but she'd motioned me down. She wasn't finished. This aunt, almost bent double with the hump on her back who moved with the aid of a walking frame.

'I felt very sorry for your mother,' she said. 'I think your mother's life really improved after your father died.' She used the arms of the chair for support as she lifted herself up slightly and readjusted the position of her back against the chair.

'Did you know my mother's mother?' I asked.

'Yes. I knew your mother's mother… Your grandmother warned your mother that they would never accept her. You can't marry him. He's Jewish and they won't accept him. What I do believe, and this will rock your boots: one Sunday morning when your grandparents lived at Coogee – up those stairs at Coogee, you had to go up the stairs – there was a slamming of doors and yelling. Your father banged the door and shouted at his father, "You mind your own business. They're my children and don't you interfere. They are my children." Then he went to talk to someone at the Temple Emanuel. Your father and grandfather didn't talk for a long time after that.'

The morning fog hovers low on the horizon. Willy wagtails bounce on the long stalks of bamboo. A quick bounce and then they fly off again. They whiz past with a motion so swift I barely see them move until the sound of their throats vibrates in song.

After a dreadful night of disjointed dreams, I'd got up and opened the curtains. The terror of the last dream was still with me. Suffocating down the bottom of a deep hole that I'd offered to dig to replant an uprooted tree. I was down the hole trying to get the roots of the large tree into place when I looked up and saw the huge dark shape of the tree looming above me. I realised that there wasn't much air left in the hole and that I'd be dead soon. I called out for help, but in a soft voice because I didn't want to use up too much oxygen. No one heard. I breathed a shallow breath, knowing I wouldn't last very long without air.

On the radio a voice says, 'I can't see the Opera House or the Bridge from where I'm standing at Circular Quay because of the fog.'

Outside the sea is flat and calm, the waves soft silent fingers of white that slowly make their way to the shore.

3

Close Hold

The Viennese waltz was the first social dance to use the 'close hold'. In the second part of the 19th century, it was considered scandalous for two people to be dancing face to face with the right arm of the man touching the back of the woman.

Tango originated before or around 1880. Here is a dance in which there is a close embrace, faces pressed cheek to cheek, chests together, the legs invading each other's space, in a long conversation of love and passion.

Alberto strides in through the door of the hall. We are waiting for him, all of us still rugged up in our coats, our dance bags on the chairs. He's been held up checking out a new venue for the dance on Saturday night. Alberto is a famous teacher of tango. He has a taut muscled body and hard arms. He wears those special dance shoes that look like sneakers, but when he points his toes, the shoes flex almost in half. Several times a week, Alberto runs classes in different parts of Sydney and, once a month, he organises a social dance, also known as a *milonga*. I am very glad that I have found my way to Alberto's lessons, although it is not easy going back to beginner classes.

My friend Nino said that Alberto has very high standards for his pupils, sometimes yelling at them, calling them hopeless and stupid because they keep making the same mistakes. Nino doesn't come to Alberto's classes any more. He's upset that some of the women think they're too good for him and step outside the circle when it's his turn to dance with them.

The hall is at the back of a church on Oxford Street, Paddington, secluded behind the church complex. I told Nino that I intend to try different classes in order to find a regular dance partner for tango.

'I don't like to go to the dances in a hall,' Nino complained. 'A church hall or a community centre or a school or wherever. I like there to be a bar so I can have a few drinks when I dance. When I first split up with my wife,' Nino said, with great understanding of my situation, 'I went out to the Apia Club, where they had a band and dancing. I asked one woman to dance, she said no. I asked another woman to dance, she said no, so I went home and watched television. The next week I went back to the Apia Club. I asked a woman to dance, she said no. I asked another woman to dance and she said no. I asked a third woman to dance. No. So I went home again and watched television. The next week, I went to the Concordia Club. I asked a woman to dance. No. Another woman. No. The third woman. Yes. We danced together and she said I danced quite well but could improve. She told me about the classes.'

Months went by in which I had no news of J. I remember at a party when he had not returned from going outside to smoke a cigarette and I decided he had met another woman. I thought it was over already, before we had been together even a week. The room seemed to empty of all sound and the people became lifeless. I couldn't hear the live band that I had been enjoying so much before. This time he had not left me, he had only gone outside to smoke a cigarette. He came back and sat next to me on a soft stool on the floor and he put his arms around me and we listened to the music of the band.

'Do you want to dance?' I asked.

'I don't dance,' he said.

'You just need to move to the music,' I reassured him. 'Nothing complicated.'

He shook his head. 'I'm too self-conscious for that.'

When I first started at Alberto's tango classes, I had trouble finding the entrance, and it was only when I saw a man and a woman in black trousers and black tops that I knew I'd come to the right place.

White plastic chairs are stacked in piles at the side of the room. There is a table on which Alberto places his sound equipment and his container of CDs. No dance bars to warm up on. The woman who arrives with Alberto is his dance partner and his girlfriend. Or that's what Nino said. Nino said they arrive together at the *milonga*s and leave together, so she must be his girlfriend. The others sit down to change into their strappy stiletto tango shoes purchased in Argentina. I'm wearing a pair of dance shoes from Bloch's with an ankle strap and a lower heel. I've had the podiatrist make a special arch support that replaces the original sole. He completely rebuilt the shoe so my body is more balanced and in alignment.

It's a small group in the class, all doing a double lesson, Beginners then Intermediate, and all experienced dancers. Each week we start by practising alone, without a partner. First the warm-up to stretch the legs and feet, the hip flexors and quads. We line up against the wall and stretch our calves and the backs of our legs. Then walking around the room. Weight on the leg then move on to it. Knees together with a slight bend, toe pointed and slightly turned out, stomach pulled up, shoulders down, toes and feet in constant contact with the floor. Then balancing.

We partner up after practising alone, all in a line. This time I'm partnered with Susan: a tall angular woman. I sense Susan trying to take control when it's my turn to lead.

'I'll close my eyes,' Susan says. 'That will help me relax.'

The downlights in the ceiling heat the skin of our hands. There's the smell of dust on the slatted blinds at the windows.

We walk forward slowly, then backwards, up and down the room. Forward and backward *ochos*. Step, swivel, step and swivel again.

'Make sure the shoulders stay to the front like they did against the wall,' Alberto instructs.

Then *giros*. Alone and then with a partner we circle around a square on the floor. Both sides, left side giro then right side *giro*. Open, step, swivel, step, open. One, two, three and four.

'Any questions at this point?' Alberto asks when the music stops.

'Do you touch the feet together on the "and" between three and four?' I ask.

'Yes,' he nods. 'Make sure that on the "and" before four, the feet touch lightly together.'

Many times, I would drive along the main road out west following J's directions to pick him up. Along that road that curves around and under the pedestrian walkway and the park on the left. I'd turn right into his street and park under a tree opposite his lounge room window. From across the road, I would sense him sitting on the couch waiting for me. Often he would appear outside with his backpack on his shoulder, ready to go with me in my car.

I stayed there only twice. The place had an awful smell that I'd noticed the first time. I couldn't identify it. Not mouldy, not cooking smells, just old smells. Smells that seemed to indicate that a lot of unpleasant things had happened there. I didn't know then that it was a halfway house. One thing I did know, because I'd asked him directly, was that there had been only a few other women, but each of them had left him.

'I'm not easy,' he said when we broke up the first time. 'No one finds me easy.'

We're practising walking the length of the hall.

Alberto says that in Buenos Aires students of tango spend two years on just learning to walk properly. 'Extend forward,' he says, 'step forward, only placing the weight on the extended leg at the last moment, toes pointed, sides of the feet staying connected to the floor.'

Then backwards with a straight leg, torso pulled up, chest up and out. And with a partner again, the connection with a partner.

'Try and choose someone the same height,' he says.

This time, I'm partnered up with a young Asian woman named Nancy. She's a tiny-framed woman so we are the same height – perfect for tango. I can smell the brightness of the washing powder on her clothes as she moves in close to me.

'Feel the connection but stay grounded, not forcing,' says Alberto. 'A conversation between two bodies to the music,' he enthuses. 'Feel the music. Really feel the music while connecting with a partner.'

J never took a photograph of me, but I know he has one taken towards the end when I felt very little for him and he was hurt by me, as I was by him, and I was doing things for him that I did not want to do, thinking that if I helped him even more things might work out. I have one photo of him taken at a fancy dress party. In this photo, his hair and eyebrows are dyed bright red, so it's not a photo I like to show people.

I used to like to go over in my mind every moment of that first time with J because the beginning was not only the first, happy occasion, opening into an infinite number of happy occasions, it also contained the end, as though the very air of that balcony where we stood together, where he leaned against me, and whispered, was already permeated with what was to follow, as though the air and the sea and the clouds were already part of the end.

By the side of the room are the dance bags and the street shoes lined up under the chairs. The ceiling fan spins above our heads; you can almost taste its steel blades, our eyes dry in their sockets.

And then the adornments. First by ourselves and then together. One toe tracing a circle on the floor. Both feet parallel as one foot goes around, out from the big toe with a circle.

'Circle, circle then step to the side.' Alberto demonstrates. His feet look like those of a ballerina even though they are encased in thick rubber.

We practise in a line behind him.

'The circle should go no farther forwards than the big toe,' he says, his foot very delicately pointed, the arch in his foot clearly defined. 'You can choose to have the knee up and trace the circle with a pointed foot, or have a flatter foot, which makes a thicker circle. The women can use the heel of their shoes rather than their toes to trace the circle.'

'You mightn't recognise me,' J had said on the phone that first time. 'I'll be wearing a jacket and tie.'

But there he was sitting up towards the back of the beer garden keeping warm under one of those metal flame heaters. I kissed him hello and inhaled peppermint, hair shampoo and cigarettes.

'I'm just sucking a breath freshener,' he said as I sat down beside him. Then he put his hand on mine. 'I've only got ten dollars on me,' he said with a look of childlike defiance, as if he expected me to challenge him. 'It's best to say it up front.'

So he only had ten dollars. That was okay. Enough for a glass of wine. And that's all I was there for. A quick drink and then I'd go home.

'What do you want?' he asked. 'Wine? I need a drink when I'm with a woman.'

So he too was nervous.

'Don't worry,' I said standing up. 'I'll get it.'

I pulled my cardigan down at the back, feeling self-conscious that he was probably watching me from behind when I walked to the bar.

When we clinked glasses, he said how nice it was to see me again. His thick eyebrows shadowed his face. 'You look nice,' he said. 'I like your necklace.'

I fingered the tiny terracotta and silver beads threaded in rows close to my neck. Velvet cord jeans, camel cardigan, high-heeled boots, chocolate wool jacket. He asked if I had any grandchildren yet, did I still live by the water? We talked about the old days in the film industry and the people we'd known and who we'd stayed in touch with and what these people were doing now. Which ones had been able to keep working in the business.

'The ones who've survived financially are the ones who've had help from their partners or from their families,' he said with envy in his tone. He wanted to show me his pilot program on the computer that was in his backpack on the floor. 'Let's go back to your place and watch it,' he said. 'Let's get another bottle and take it with us. I'll pay you back.'

The fan is reflected in the two mirrors, one mirror directly opposite the other mirror. Ceiling fans in mirrors, on and on, into infinity.

'Find something to put on the floor that is the shape of a square,' instructs Alberto.

I take the *Sydney Morning Herald* out of my handbag and fold it in half. Other people find pieces of paper or even their street shoes to use as a marker. Nancy and I square up and then we begin. We circle the square on the floor, making sure to keep our shoulders parallel to each other. We take turns being the person who decides it's time for a change of direction from left side *giro* to right side *giro*. Who will lead and who will follow?

I told my friends that the women at tango aren't very friendly. Well, two are, two aren't. One was, but isn't any more. That first week, when we'd been partnered up for one of the exercises, Susan had seemed quite nice. We'd walked to our cars together after the lesson and she'd asked if I was coming to the dance on Saturday night. But some of the women are such bitches. Like Cynthia and Rosemary and Tina and the other aggressive women who come up and take a man right out from under your nose. You'll be having a conversation, about to dance together, and they come up without even waiting for a pause in the conversation and ask the man to dance.

J held my hand as we walked to the car. The side of the road was brightly lit by street lights and floodlights around the hotel. The other side of the road was dark, lined with trees that shaded the road from the electric lights. Power lines intersected between the leaves. I asked him to drive, me being the nervous driver that I am. He strapped himself in to the driver's seat after first handing me the seat belt. He waited until I clicked myself in.

Back at my place, we settled back on the couch and watched his video. It was an introduction to a series he wanted to produce. Just a piece to camera, that was all. His arm was along the back of the couch behind me. Beyond our reflection in the window, a storm approached from the east. There was the thud of thunder. The horizon seemed dulled and dampened. White waves against a dark sea.

'How old are you?' he asked.

'You know how old my kids are, so you can guess.'

'You're not that much older than me,' he estimated.

'A fair bit older. Fourteen years older.'

I got up then and pulled back the sliding door and went out onto the terrace, where the air was thick with the smell of the sea. He followed me out and moved up behind me and nestled his face into the back of my neck. I held onto the balcony as he pressed against me, felt the force of him from behind, the coolness of the steel railing against my stomach. He kissed my hair, the side of my neck, and I leant back into him. The wind whistled up the gully. Distant thunder. His mouth soft, gently probing with his tongue. A flash of lightning out to sea. Thunder, louder this time, crackled the sky.

We moved into the bedroom. I worried about the brightness of the light next to the bed near my face. His fingers were in the loops of my clothes. He didn't bother undressing. The sweet moist smell of rain. Another flash of lightning. The thunderclaps louder and deeper and broader in spectrum. His eyes were closed. The rain gathered momentum. Pounded the railing of the balcony. It kept on. Constant and relentless.

He was good.

A huge empty space. Hollow footsteps at the end of the day. A glimpse of green through glass. The rain that has been hovering all afternoon fills the gutters and pours down the drainpipes and makes the leaves on the trees bend down from the weight of it all. The breeze feels cool through the flyscreens. The phone rings. It's Alberto to say the *milonga* will be at the North Sydney RSL on Saturday night.

'What do you think will be the proportion of men to women?' I ask.

'More men.'

'I don't want to sit like a wallflower,' I moan. 'It's bad for my self-esteem.'

'Don't worry,' he says. 'I'll dance with you. I'll dance with you so much that you'll be too tired to dance with anyone else.'

I laugh when he says that. It really makes me laugh. I really do laugh.

4

J.

In solitude we give passionate attention to our lives, to our memories, to the details around us. – Virginia Woolf

This morning I sprayed my plants with a fungicide. On the label it said the fungicide will have a curative action on disease. There are holes in the leaves of the plants and their stems are covered with a powdery mildew that seems to mirror my own spreading inertia – contaminating myself and everything around me.

Lethargy is beginning to envelop me. The time in front of me stretches out endlessly, as if both the day and I are under a thick cloud. It might be the thought of the coming summer and the humidity that makes me think I must get away for a short time, as a normal person would. The leaves have grown back on the trees, the days are getting longer, the mornings brighter.

Outside the window, two birds with yellow beaks chatter and peck at the knotty slope of the branch of a tree. Distant motorised noises, perhaps a digger, but otherwise I'm conscious of being alone and totally undisturbed. There are no telephone calls or telephone messages to be answered, which is good, although I hadn't expected any. There is no logic to the way I am working now. I don't know what I'm doing or where it's all going. The fear and self-loathing set in, as they always do. Perhaps it's the silence of this apartment that makes me think that elsewhere will be different and better. But I know that a great effort of will will be needed if I'm to go anywhere.

The sun begins its climb from behind a bunch of grey gorged

clouds. First the top third and then the whole orange ball appears. Its warmth is brief before the clouds cover its brightness.

I remember with a smile the last time I saw my friend Annalyse. We'd gone out to a café for coffee and cake.

'I wrote a paragraph today,' I'd boasted.

She'd laughed.

'What's so funny?' I said.

She looked so pretty wearing the blue and turquoise glass necklace and drop earrings that I'd given her for her birthday, her shiny moss-green blouse, her dear face with its chiselled features completely devoid of makeup.

'That you wrote one paragraph today,' she'd said pushing the cheesecake towards me. She wiped her mouth with the corner of a serviette then asked, 'How are you coping with the break-up with J?'

'I'm still praying for a miracle.'

She shook her head. 'What?' She frowned. 'That he hasn't got a mental illness?'

'That's the thing,' I'd lamented. 'I thought it wouldn't matter.'

A light breeze stirs the leaves. Seven lorikeets bounce on the branches of the tree, made more brilliant by the early morning light and the bright sky.

Just as J looked a little different to me each time we met, I also learned new things about him. Each thing I learned came as a small surprise, and either pleased me or shocked me, and disturbed me a little or a great deal.

In the beginning, I paid such close attention to what I saw when he would first appear, what was different about him from what I had last seen, that I remember his clothes with surprising clarity. What I saw was not only his face, not only his hands, and not just the position of his body, but also his steel-grey wool jacket, crushed at the back, his maroon collarless shirt, his beige cord trousers, and his khaki lace-up boots. I never did get the smell of his clothes out of my cupboard.

There was a strong odour of the man before me in the room when I first walked in. Dr Ross lowered the blinds on the windows that faced the west, then sat down, his pen poised, his notebook on his lap. I wanted to ask for a window to be opened but after a while I got used to the smell of the room and became part of it.

'I was so stupid,' I said.

'You can't just roll your life back to the beginning as if it's a film,' he counselled. 'You gave it a lot of consideration. You didn't do it lightly. You did what seemed the right thing under the circumstances. You might not still be with him now anyway if you'd stayed together then. Who knows what might have happened? Everyone thinks about the "what ifs". That's why so many people are on Prozac.'

'I wish it wasn't like this.'

'Life *is* like this. Life is monotonous. That's the way it is. People have to get up early in the mornings, go to work, take the kids to school.'

'Now I think that I could have tried harder. Could have made it work.'

'You didn't have a chance.'

A bird flies over the leafy skull of a tree. A gentle breeze moves the curtains, the mid-morning light dulled already as the sun moves behind the building. The rocks by the surf club are licked then lapped by the waves that engulf then retreat from their moist round surfaces. I have to remember to keep looking at the sea. Soon the foliage of the giant bamboo will grow up again and block the view and the light. The waves break far out and I can see a whole long line of waves, riding in tandem towards the cliffs and the beach. The woman upstairs said there used to be echidnas in this gulley before the bamboo and noxious weeds took over.

The new handyman is so punctual that I'm still in my dressing gown when he arrives, my hair caught up with combs, and I just have time to put on some red lipstick to keep from looking as disgusting as

I feel. I'm sorry about the way I look even more when I open the door and see that he's not a crusty old bloke, as I thought he would be, but a young man carrying a blue plastic milk crate full of tools. Screwdrivers of different colours are slung low in a belt around his hips. His shirt is short-sleeved, perfect for Sydney's unpredictable spring and windy but rainless days.

He hands me his card and says I look familiar. 'Are you one of Australia's Most Wanted?' he jokes.

I wonder if he dances. Maybe that's where he's seen me.

'I have one of those familiar faces,' I say. 'I go into shops and people say, "Weren't you in here yesterday trying on all the clothes?" No, I wasn't, but I look like the person who was in the shop yesterday.'

While he's setting up his black three-step ladder, he asks me how was my weekend.

'Good.'

'Don't you find it's the same old, same old, sometimes?'

'I try to keep the variety happening.'

He moves my desk away from the sliding glass door in order to scrape down the frame, forcing me to sit on the bed rather than at the desk by the window. I'm preparing the apartment for sale; getting a few things fixed up, replacing the rusted curtain tracks and the chipped paint around the doors, and the rusted security grills. He's fixed the rusty grills on the kitchen window, repainted the chipped frames around the sliding glass door and removed the ugly black fixtures on the wall of the laundry. 'Cheap at half the price,' he'd reassured me with a pat on the shoulder when I'd asked him for a quote to come back and paint the rusted security bars.

I try to work as his scraper makes a rhythmic banging and his sandpaper scratches. He uses a dry paintbrush to remove the surplus bits of paint and then his dustpan and brush to clean up the door track. There he is on his hands and knees sweeping up the bits.

We chat about the usefulness of milk crates as he makes his way to the front door, his tools back in the blue plastic container. When I hand him the cheque, he says he's going out that night to have a drink with his mates.

'Not a lot of drinking goes on at the clubs where I go to dance,' I say. 'Ballroom dancers don't drink much.'

'It's the reverse of the usual,' he says with respect in his tone. 'People usually get drunk, and then wobble around a bit.'

Forcing myself up out of the chair by the window, I walk into the kitchen, open the lid of the kettle, pour some water in, turn on the switch, reach for a mug, find a tea bag, tip the water on top, sit back down, look out to the sea.

I'm remembering telling Annalyse the story of Pedro, my new dance partner. How each week he chews the gum so sedately, no moving of the jaws, but always a nice fresh mouth, our faces so close. He'd sucked a mint that other Saturday night when he'd escorted me home on the train in preparation for the kiss he never received.

'Dancing forces men to clean their teeth and to keep themselves nice,' said my friend Gareth.

'It's really important to smell good,' I said.

'I don't wear aftershave to the lessons because I don't want to give the wrong impression,' Gareth said, sipping a cup of tea during the break.

But then I'd had to reprimand him when he came to the lesson reeking of the dinner he'd bought on the run. 'They put a lot of garlic in takeaway food,' I'd said, pulling away from him.

'You must be very sensitive to smell.'

Pedro always smells, or rather, smelt, nice. Past-tense Pedro. I don't intend to put myself in that position again.

'He's mad,' Nino had warned. 'Pedro is mad. People see him saying those things to you that don't relate to the dancing. Non-Latins see it and think things.'

'I don't give a damn what people think about me and Pedro,' I wanted to say. But the image of Pedro with his hands around that woman's waist and Pedro asking that bitch if she'd like a drink remains vividly in my mind and in my heart. And now my heart smells like a bit of cast off offal.

And that other rude man who'd said, 'Your perfume has given me a headache. What perfume do you use?' he'd asked with his pale face and his shiny high forehead.

'Why?' I'd frowned, already suspecting he wasn't about to say something nice. 'Are you allergic to it?'

I almost went home then, but I'd waited for Pedro. And then Pedro, to carry on like that because he'd assumed I was going away to the mountains with a man.

'A honeymoon?' he'd accused before turning to the woman with the black hair and a wedding ring on her ugly knuckle.

And then, at that moment, there was Alfonse beckoning me from across the room.

'Me?' I queried. 'Do you mean me?'

Dear sweet Alfonse practising his hooks and *ganchos* as we'd pressed and leant and released and swivelled. He'd smelt nice because he was there with his new girlfriend. The girlfriend who made it very clear where I stood.

'Alfonse is very young,' she said. 'That's why I encouraged him to dance with you. I told him to dance with you. I did it deliberately.'

Pigeons and seagulls scavenge for food on the grass. One pigeon steps forward, his lilac chest expanding. There are flashes of lime green as he nibbles and nips at his wings. A breeze moves through the grass.

'It was late on a wet Tuesday night when Pedro finally came over to invite me to dance. He'd approached from behind like he usually does when I'm not expecting it. I'd seen him arrive and dance with Margery first, then that young attractive Chinese woman, and then someone else, I can't remember who. I'd tried not to watch because it only makes me jealous, but I would have liked to see what he looked like, or what other women looked like, when they dance with him. Annalyse, I don't want him, but I don't want anyone else to have him. He has this way of dancing – it's very intimate, you know how they are?'

'The groper,' Annalyse said.

'"It's good you came in the pouring rain," I said to him. "I thought you mightn't come." "I've got an umbrella," he said, surprised. "No problem if you've got an umbrella." Nino says Pedro is like a wild cat the way he stalks his prey before pouncing. But then Pedro calls Nino an old man. "What are you doing with such an old man?" he used to say when Nino still danced with me. "Make sure your batteries are charged," he'd call out to Nino. Alfredo. You know Alfredo. That mad look in his eyes. I don't know what's wrong with him, I'd said to Alfredo, "You're a Latin. You understand him better than I do." "Is he senile?" Alfredo suggested. Of course not, I said, rolling my eyes.'

'We're tango crazies,' said Annalyse. 'All crazy about tango.'

'Later, when a lot of people had left and the place had emptied out, when Pedro and I were one of the only couples left, he asked if I'd give him a lift to the station. Yes, I said, without hesitation this time. "Good," he said pulling me closer. He licked the perspiration off the side of my face and sighed. Then we danced a *vals*. Anyway, I was so keyed up I made a mistake and went into the cross when I should have stepped to the side. "I'm sorry," I said. "I must be getting tired. I'm losing my concentration." "Don't say sorry," he whispered in my ear. "Just say, I love you." He pulled me even closer and altered the position of my body in front of his. I was slightly to the left, like in ballroom, but now I was directly in front of him.'

'What happened after that?' asked Annalyse, her voice rising in pitch. 'It would be wonderful…oh Sofia,' she pleaded. 'It would be wonderful to have it all in the one person. The dancing and a relationship.'

'When we left the club, he had his umbrella up and insisted we shelter under the one umbrella and he used his arm on my shoulder to make sure I didn't get wet. "I'm sorry I'm touching you on the shoulder," he said as a joke. "You're a funny man," I laughed.'

'How old is he?
'My age.'
'I thought he'd be young. Like J.'
'So that's all. Nothing else. I dropped Pedro at the station and went home.'

*

Beyond the car park and the tiled suburban roofs lie the Blue Mountains spreading out across the horizon. The dense cloud sometimes vanishes without warning to reveal the spectacular sandstone cliffs and waterfalls of the Jameson Valley.

'It's a good time to go to the mountains,' Annalyse had encouraged when I'd rung to say goodbye.

From the window, all I can see is a retreating area of grey, the mountain mist engulfing the peaks of the Three Sisters. I turn my back on the thick grey expanse beyond the window, and look around the room. Beige and blue chequered cover on the broad queen-sized bed, matching chequered curtains, parted with bright red sashes and a narrow white-painted wardrobe with three drawers. But the drawers of the dresser are jammed closed by the nearness of the other furniture and the side wall.

Very soon, I will unpack and go downstairs and have a cup of tea. The place seems deserted, although people are probably resting in their rooms, having a body treatment, or out walking. I go over to the bed, lean back, close my eyes, then lean further back against the pillows. I lie there for a few minutes, then take a deep breath. Tea. I need a nice hot cup of tea. And then a walk, a long walk into the town, and then a shower, and then change into something to wear for the Egyptian sacred dancing, and after that I'll be ready for a nice gourmet vegetarian dinner. And after that I will sit in the lounge and listen to the talk, 'Angels and You'. I need an early night. In fact, I'm very tired already. The yawn, when it comes, sounds like a suffocated scream.

Unpacking takes only a few minutes. I carry the creams and oils into the bathroom, slip the key into my pocket and step out into the corridor, fragrant with lavender and geranium. Walking down the wide, shallow stairs, I can hear laughter echoing from the lounge where women wait to be called to their treatments.

A tall woman holds forth, her smooth brown skin revealed in a sleeveless top, her thick white nails cut horizontally at the tips, her big gold rings and matching gold necklace glittering in the glow of the fire. As the woman sweeps her bleached blonde hair off her forehead, I notice one white nail is missing and in its place is a nicotine-stained nail stub bitten down even lower than the quick.

'Here I am,' says a voice, and into the room comes a young woman.

'There you are, darling,' says the woman, who must be her mother. 'I've just finished. Did you get an appointment?'

'No, but it doesn't matter,' says the girl, who is, I see, a paler version of her mother.

'But darling,' exclaims the older woman, 'you must get an appointment. That's why we came. They can surely fit you in somewhere.'

The younger woman says something else to her mother, using her hands for emphasis, palms turned upwards, then both hands towards her heart as she leans forward.

'Do something with yourself,' says the mother. 'Go and do the course. Go and learn something. Get yourself occupied.'

'Yeah…'

'Don't be depressed like Susanna. You're a smart person, you shouldn't be doing this.'

'I try and put myself in your and Dad's shoes.'

'Love someone that you'd do anything for,' the mother says, putting her arms around her daughter, who moves into them and snuggles her face against her mother's shoulder.

'Ah,' the older woman laughs. 'You're lucky you've got me, aren't you, darling?'

They embrace and then walk to the door, still entwined. I feel a pang of wistfulness for my own daughter as I watch them walk away. My daughter who hadn't wanted to spend a weekend away, just the two of us. She'd said we make each other tense if we're together too much. But she'd said it in a kind voice.

'You don't mind, do you?' she'd asked.

I did mind. 'At least you're honest with me,' I said.

Now I watch the mother and daughter in their identical black hipster trousers, a flash of flesh between top and bottom, high heels on the older woman, white joggers on the daughter, the girl's ponytail swinging behind her.

I walk through the silent lobby, through the glass-paned front door, across the road and up the hill in the fading light of the grey day. The silence engulfs me as I go past the town's one intersection, and it seems as if I might walk forever, uninterrupted, with only my thoughts for company.

It was the week before J's thirty-eighth birthday that we'd met. He'd just quit work at a hotel in Kings Cross. He'd been there six months, sweeping the paths and doing the odd bit of maintenance work. He didn't like the work but even so it took an argument with the manager to get him out of there. But anyway, he had people to see, places to go, and appointments to make in relation to the television program he was trying to get up and running.

When he gave the job up, all he had left was his computer, a bicycle and a room in a two-bedroom unit at Leichhardt. He said the place was a bit of a mess until they moved Manny in with him a couple of weeks later. The floor was covered with piles of credit card receipts, stacks of pink overdraft notices from the banks, and duplicate and triplicate billings from all of the stores through which he'd charged. There was a separate, more ominous pile with its threatening letters from collection agencies.

Manny was good at getting things in order, filling the fridge with food, getting a load of washing on. A woman friend said that living with Manny would help J to know what it's like to be around someone like him.

'You'll find out what your friends have to put up with,' she'd said.

J knew that if he could like Manny then maybe he could like himself too. He called him Mad Manny.

J said, 'As for me, I could have said that things were under control, but who was I to say? I didn't know any more who was the real me.'

In J's head, he had a spectrum: at one end he was working as a producer or cinematographer back in the world of words and pictures; at the other, he was homeless and friendless walking the streets. 'My greatest fear was, and still is, being alone and out on the street,' he'd said.

His unit was in an old apartment block, dark brick, leadlight doors. The other residents had been in Rozelle Hospital, were single, and lived on benefits. To occupy themselves, they'd spend their time drinking tea or cheap wine, and watching television in each other's rooms.

The only important difference between the eight of them was how likely it was that any of them would get out of there. With some, you could tell it would never happen; with others, like Daniel, the guy across the hallway, it seemed possible. Although he rarely left his unit, except to go to the garage to buy cigarettes and milk, he had the support of his girlfriend, Rosa. The plan was that they'd get jobs and then move into a place together.

Rosa had Daniel on a budget and doled money out to him small bits at a time. She stayed over most weekends. The sad thing was that she hadn't told her family about Daniel. She had grown-up children and he was only twenty-nine, or maybe the reason she didn't tell her family was because they'd met at Rozelle Psychiatric.

Making my way back through the twilight, I see the hotel from afar, lit up, white and welcoming. In the silent foyer, the lights are very bright, there's a mumble of voices from the kitchen and the smell of tofu and brown rice. I go upstairs to my room.

I sit on the bed for a long time, the room now totally silent. I'm not aware of time passing. Instead, I look back into the past, to other silent times. I find myself thinking about the mother and daughter I'd seen together in the lounge. I think about their embrace, their arms locked around each other. There was love there, love between mother and daughter, and physical contact. I'd never had that with my own mother. My own puzzling mother, that bitter, disappointed woman.

Once, as a child, I came running into her bedroom. I saw her sitting at her dressing table. She was wearing that white silk blouse and long shiny black beads, and was quite still, looking at herself in the mirror with her hands resting in her lap. I went up to her. She gave me a look so full of sadness that I nearly burst into tears. But instead I stroked her on the back. She closed her eyes and let me do it.

Suddenly she came to herself and said, 'Is that you who's been into my cupboards snooping through my things when I'm at work?'

The heat rose up in my chest, my neck and then into my face. The slap, when it came, was well placed, edged like steel. And then, just as suddenly, she began to weep. Her face changed again and, giving her strange laugh, she wiped her eyes.

'How foolish of me' was all that she said. She got up and left me standing there in my confusion.

In a dream, I'd been to visit Mother and Father at home. Mother was immaculately groomed in a beautiful paisley ensemble and high-heeled shoes with pointy toes. Father was wearing a pair of crisp trousers and a freshly ironed shirt. He seemed like his old self – not sick at all. Mother announced that they were going for a fish lunch and a walk by the sea. A tentative happiness settled on me. Mother and Father were together and everything seemed to be all right.

When I woke up in the dark room, I was crying. There was a finger of grey through the curtains as I lay there waiting for the sound of the birds and the light of the dawn to appear. I counted slowly. One, two, three on the in-breath, one, two, three on the out-breath, until I noticed that water was lapping up and into the bedroom.

I'm imagining J that day just before we met when he'd resigned from his job at the hotel. He rode his bike home, stopped at the garage to buy a packet of chocolate cream mint biscuits, then walked up the front steps into the hall. Daniel's door was open. He looked in. Daniel was sitting with Rosa in front of the television. He had his arm around her on the couch.

'J,' Rosa called out. 'Come in here!'

She was eyeing off the packet of biscuits he was carrying. He declined. He had to do some serious thinking about the TV drama and how to get it off the ground. He wanted the biscuits for himself.

His room was at ground level. He unlocked the door and closed it behind him, parked the bicycle in the hallway, threw his jumper onto the pile in the bedroom, turned the kitchen light on and recoiled as the cockroaches scuttled into the dark corners. He scrummaged for a mug in the sink.

He took the biscuits into the lounge, took one out, and sat there for a time; rested his arm on the cool blue linen of the chair, then leant forward and snatched up the mug. He recoiled as his lips met the cold scum that had formed on the coffee's surface. Beyond his reflection in the window, his world seemed to have shrunk.

He got up and padded across to the bathroom; stared at his face in the mirror above the toilet, ran his hand up through his hair. At least I still look good, he thought. No doubt I can thank my Spanish mother for that.

The mirror was above the bathroom cabinet. Manny said he'd leave the cabinet for J to clean up. Manny kept his toothbrush and toothpaste in his bedroom as a protest at the state of the shelves in the cabinet.

J lit a cigarette and turned on the television.

It was a Wednesday night. Having time to get on with the project seemed fine, but he'd have to find himself another job to earn some money. Money was the thing. He could go back on benefits but it hardly covered the cost of cigarettes. He thought about maybe, despite it all, getting up and looking for work the next day. But damn it, he wouldn't need to get a job if he could get the TV thing happening.

'He sounds like he was a user,' Dr Ross had said. 'He met you. You've got your own home, you're achieving with your work, you do what you say you'll do. He thought, this is for me. I'll get in on this one.'

'He said he felt safe with me. He talked about us living together.'

'As soon as he met you?'

'No. Not straight away.'

'He probably thought you'd pay off his debts.'

'I'm not that stupid.'

'You've got the freedom to do whatever you like,' Dr Ross added, before throwing the box of tissues towards me. He turned his writing pad over with a loud snap against his knees.

The rattling of the wind in the windowpanes wakes me up again. Sitting up cautiously in the unfamiliar bed, I look at my watch to try to see the time. It must be very early. I remember waking during the night and hearing the wind through the building. I lie there reflecting on the previous evening. Well, at least I'd achieved something. I'd joined in the Egyptian sacred dancing and it hadn't been too bad and at least the women are beginning to have names. And the talk on angels in the lounge had ambled on aimlessly but luckily I'd taken a book to read.

I get up and pull the curtains then stand at the window. I can see a storm coming in, rolling across the escarpment. All around the dark ridge, the mist has deepened into large thickened clouds. The first of the rain starts to fall as I watch. I'd heard the windows straining against their sashes last night just like in the old house where I'd lived when I was a child. The rattling of the old windows and the doors that brought a sense of dread. The roof would leak and Mother would get out the buckets to collect the water. Another thing that Father couldn't get right. Couldn't even provide a proper roof over our heads. And then the two of them would start up again.

Out of the sparkling breeze of September – the midday north-easterlies that flapped the green flags on the boat flagpoles and blew them in a uniform direction, waiting and hoping for spring's calming influence – appeared the caramel shape, first the backless swimming costume, then the denim shorts, then the rest of the body of Mother. Her red plastic flip-flops progressed along the shore of the beach. I couldn't say with any certainty if I was with her, but she didn't walk very far, not with her feet flecked with salt, one or two grey curls escaping from under her peaked cap, not with her face rigid as fine porcelain, unguarded. She stepped under a tree and eased herself back on an aluminium chair. Her fine gold necklace lay in the deep crevice of her chest, the same colour as the dangerous lichen-covered rocks.

I get up, shake out my hair, pick up the key and leave the room. As I walk towards the stairs, there is a rosy scent mixed with stewed apples and porridge. The weather has calmed down, the winds waning, as if releasing their hold so that the light of the day can grow stronger. Once again, the mountains are emerging through the mist.

Subdued music plays in the dining room with its round tables for eight, its white cloths over apricot cotton, a buffet of food along one wall in front of a mural of a misty valley with waratahs and frangipanis, parrots and cockatoos. I sit down at one of these tables with a group of women. All women. Only women. J. Oh, J.

He'd switched the heater on and then reached down under the coffee table and pulled out the two photograph albums. It was only then when he showed me a picture of the film crew from a shoot in Adelaide that I'd realised we had been part of the same crew. I saw the photo of everyone else working on the documentary sitting in a church pew and realised I must have been the one who took the photo.

He turned the pages of the album to pictures of his first photographic exhibition when he was eighteen, his hair so long that I hardly recognised him.

'I mounted and lit the exhibition myself,' he said proudly.

I looked at his photos of the people and the landscapes in the small country town where he'd grown up. He told me about his alcoholic father who worked in a coal mine and his mother who became a radio journalist.

'I've got some other photos in an album in my room of Belinda and Alison,' he said.

'I don't want to see pictures of your old girlfriends.'

He raised his eyebrows at me. 'Why not?'

I shook my head. 'I don't want to see them. Are you still doing freelance camera work?' I asked.

'I sold all my camera gear,' J sighed. 'I wanted to put a deposit on a place. I really want to settle down, to buy a house, have a family.'

'Children?'

'I've always wanted to have children,' he said, 'since I was in my twenties, but the women I lived with wouldn't have them with me. What about you? Do you think you'll have any more children?'

'My kids are grown up,' I said, 'and live in their own houses.'

'Did you have a treatment yesterday?' asks the woman seated beside me at the round table.

'No. It sounds silly, but I walked into Katoomba and went to Medicare to make some claims.'

The woman laughs. 'People will say to you, "What did you do on your holiday?" "I went to Medicare," you can tell them.'

'What treatments did you have yesterday?'

'A facial and a pedicure and then an aromatherapy bath before I went to bed,' she says, wrapping a muffin in a serviette to take to her room. 'I saw you at the talk on angels last night. Reading a book behind the handout. That's the sort of thing we used to do at school.'

Well, I'd joined in at least, sat there with the others in the lounge. 'Have you been here before?' I ask.

'Twice before and both times I was on a fast. Recovering from glandular fever.'

'What was it like, being on a fast?'

'After the first couple of days, you don't crave food. You don't have that empty feeling. Your body goes into starvation mode and feeds off itself. But every time you look at the television or open a magazine, you see an ad for food and that makes you think of how much you enjoy eating. The fast is an inward journey. You stay in your room a lot because that's all you feel like doing. You sleep a lot. Maybe join a class or go to a talk. Read. I wrote in my diary because you focus in on yourself. I felt like writing.'

Around the table, the conversation gets on to sex, sex and marriage, sex and the single life.

'Marriage is one long monotony,' contributes one woman.

'If they're single, we wonder, how often are they doing it? And with whom? Is he or she good in bed, whatever that means?'

I remember a quote by Auden and decide to make a contribution to the discussion. 'W.H. Auden once described sexual craving as an intolerable neural itch.'

There are nods and sniggers and exclamations of agreement.

Then, from across the table, a curvaceous woman in a black plunging shoestring top tells us she believes in the power of witchcraft. 'Witchcraft is one of the few mystical paths where sensuality and sexuality go hand in hand,' she says. 'I have a shower, light some mint incense, stand naked in front of the mirror and say, "You are a goddess, your body is your temple," then do deep breathing exercises.'

No one comments.

'I'm a great tree-hugger,' adds the woman, now enthusiastic about sharing a little more of herself and her ideas. 'Whenever I see a tree, I hug it.'

'Whatever for?'

'I'm saying hello to the spirit who lives inside.'

'Then what?'

'It picks me up. Gives me energy.' She dabs the corners of her mouth. 'Friends nagged me to find a soulmate, so I filled my glass with crushed ice and sliced orange and wrote down the words "I am ready". I bit the orange, focused on the ice and within two hours Gianfranco walked through the door. Six months later, we married.'

The only sound is cutlery scraping against china.

He'd yawned. 'I've just done ten hours of hard physical labour, mopping thirty lots of stairs,' J said. 'But I've been able to organise some meetings over the next couple of weeks. I've even bought a diary,' he said, sounding very pleased with himself.

'I couldn't live without a diary,' I said. 'But I'm a well-organised person.'

'And I'm a very disorganised person, as you've probably noticed.'

'Well, look in your diary and see if you're free next Saturday night.'

'I don't need to look. I can remember what I've got on.'

'It's a birthday party. A big-0 celebration.'

'A fortieth?'

'Yes,' I lied.

At the party, I introduced J to Louise and her husband. We put the wine on the bench in the kitchen where the other bottles were, and accepted a glass of punch. The party developed. J took to it well. He was young, looked good, and he'd worked in the film business. They were impressed. He moved around, talking, laughing, chatting to the women who approached him. They asked him where he'd met me and he said we used to work together.

In the morning, I got up out of bed and went into the kitchen to make him a cup of tea. I'd left the bedroom curtains open because he'd said he'd wanted to see the dawn. He watched as I placed the teacup on the table beside the bed. I'd slept badly. He'd been snoring and calling out in his sleep. The increase in medication made him like that. The sound of light rain was in the trees, water dripping from the unit above on to the side of the balcony. When I got back into bed, he curled up against me, reached down, ran his hand up between my legs. I rolled towards him. The sun, between mountainous grey clouds, shone in on to his face.

'Your eyelashes are beautiful,' I said. 'And your skin. It's so soft.'

I still thought, even though I knew it was over, that I might visit him at the place where he worked, but although I heard no news of him, I decided not to try to get in touch. That last cup of tea, the last tea bag in the box of one hundred was a definitive act, as though drinking the last tea bag from the box became the end. And, since all along there have been many ends to our story, and since the story didn't end for me, but only continued something, something that I have not spoken about, I needed a definitive act to end the story of J.

So it is that I became aware that (i) I had not got to the bottom of something, and (ii) that I was not being completely honest with myself.

The scent of lavender from the oil burner as the massage progresses. The masseur starts with firm but relaxing manipulation of the feet, then the chest, neck, face and head. We chat about this and that during the treatment until somehow we get on to the topic of sex.

'Men over fifty aren't interested in sex any more,' she says in an authoritative voice. 'They become lazy. It's too much of an effort and men go through a menopause at fifty just like women do. After menopause, women's sexual appetite decreases and so does men's. But you don't hear about it because women aren't going to say they have no sex because they worry that people will think their husbands have lost interest in them – that they don't find them attractive any more.'

She talks about her divorce and said she remarried after only eight months on her own. 'I was having a ball,' she says as she tissues the cream off my face. 'I didn't expect that I'd fall in love again, but I did. And you never remarried?'

'No. I do think about it. I miss having an intimate relationship with a man.'

'There's no intimacy if you are with a man.'

'What do you mean?'

'No sex. Once they get to fifty, they lose interest.'

'Really? I didn't know that. Although a married friend said to me recently that sex is a distant memory for men and women our age. I was shocked. I didn't know. No one says that. You don't read about it in articles or in novels.'

'People don't talk about it. I only know because I see so many people in the intimate setting of a treatment room. People talk in this setting and I hear it all the time.'

'So the women still want sex and the men don't?'

'That's right. The men think it's too much trouble. Although it's not always the case. My cousin's husband died at seventy-three while having sex – or just after. He always said it was the way he'd want to go. He still liked to have sex every three days. But it was a mechanical thing with him. He'd just climb on and that was it.'

'Is it because the men can't get erections any more – impotent?'

'No. They're just not interested. You get more sex as a single person.'

'You mean have flings?'

'Yes. Go out and do what feels good. What are you saving it for? Sleep with them on the first date if you want to. If it feels good, do it. That's what I tell my daughters. My husband's shocked. He's very old-fashioned.'

After breakfast, the bell rings to announce it's time for the guided walk.

'Look at the different colours of the light in the valley today,' says the guide as we step over tree roots and slippery lumps of stone.

He leads us along a path that winds down the cliff face, taking us into the valley. Safe in a cool silent cove, we view the world through a curtain of fine water.

It reminds me of those journeys you take in a dream, in which confusion and clarity go hand in hand. The muted tones of the bush, too, are that of a dream, a patchwork of shapes neither in full colour or in stark black and white.

We keep going, moving forward along the dirt tracks and down the steps towards the smell of mossy stone.

Unable to restrain myself, I'd asked J about Ellen. 'Have you slept with her?'

'What?' J said. 'No!'

'Why not?' I persisted.

He looked at me. 'Because I don't want to.'

He got out of bed wearing only his underpants, reached for his woollen blazer, put his bare arms through the sleeves and went out to the balcony to light up. I could see him through the glass door. He was gazing out to sea and drawing deeply on his cigarette.

I was worrying already about him going home and when I'd see him again, so I asked, 'When will I see you again? I'd like to see you soon.'

He exhaled out towards the ocean, the smoke drifting over the stalks of bamboo. 'Likewise,' he said. 'You can come to the Bewitched party at Ellen's house tonight if you want to. We'll just be watching television but you can come with me and stay the night.'

'Where will I sleep? You usually sleep in one of the kid's rooms.'

'You'll sleep with me. Ellen's got a divan in the lounge that converts into a double bed, although it's probably not very comfortable.'

'That's okay,' I said.

He came back in from the balcony, took his jacket off, hopped back into bed. He nestled his head into my hair. 'You're very accepting,' he said.

'Just keep taking the tablets.'

He'd said he planned to spend his weekends helping Ellen renovate her house. 'This will give structure to my week.'

We were sitting together at a wooden coffee table in an outside courtyard in a café. Either we were on our way to see a movie or we were simply trying to finish our quarrel. The moon shone down at an angle and reflected off the uneven bricks covering the soil on the ground and faded palings of the fence, and because the trees were sparse with leaves, a great expanse of dark grey sky was visible.

'Helping Ellen to renovate her house is such a big job,' I said. I could see it stretching out indefinitely.

This café where we sat was famous for its gelatos. J said something about the gelatos we'd eaten together when we walked across the Sydney Harbour Bridge. I said we've never eaten gelatos together. That's when he realised it was him and Ellen, not him and me.

'Are you in love with Ellen?' I asked. 'Or something like that.'

He frowned. 'No. I'm not in love with Ellen.'

On the track, we pass a couple of tourists examining a map where the track splits around huge stones then drops through the bushes to a lower path. We walk back along the valley rim then stand at a lookout where the faded colours of the mountains merge into the blue haze.

The first break-up was on J's birthday. He said later his father had died on that day many years earlier and that had made it particularly hurtful for him. The second break-up was when he'd found it necessary to pay me back for hurting him so much the first time.

It was raining at the end of a cloudless day when the noise of the rain on the bamboo drowned the rhythmic murmur of the sea. When we finally got back to my place, I'd gone to my room and lain on the bed. He stayed in the lounge finishing a second bottle. Two willy wagtails flew past the window as I'd watched. They were lit from beneath by the remains of the day's sunshine. The air felt crisp through the door, the sky above the horizon tinged with mauve. A gust of wind rustled the stalks of bamboo, making a faint whooshing sound, as if the wind was waiting to exhale. The windows were shadowed with dusk and vibrated in the wind.

'Why don't you kiss me hello on the lips when you say hello?' he'd asked. 'That's what girlfriends do, isn't it?'

I hadn't put my arms around him when he arrived at the door, hadn't felt the texture of his jacket, or the contours of his body, didn't touch his hair or run my hand along the skin at the back of his neck.

At a café near Katoomba train station, with its clouded windows now transparent and bathed in afternoon light, a man grinds black pepper onto his scrambled eggs, sausages, baked beans, Turkish toast, fried mushrooms and grilled tomato halves. He scoops up mouthfuls of baked beans and mushrooms into his mouth, spreads butter on his Turkish toast while sipping at his latte and glancing out the window.

'I'll close up and bring the TV down for the big game and put it on the table here near the window,' says the owner of the café to the man.

'Will you have a big screen?' asks the man.

'You ask too many questions, mate,' says the owner. 'Like a sheila,' he says, swiping the air in a negative fashion.

I close my eyes momentarily in a shaft of sunlight.

After five days, J had stopped trying to phone and a different kind of bleakness had closed down around me. First anger, then relief, then hope, then despair, then anger again, and I had to struggle to keep track of where I was. Anger at myself, anger with him, anger with life. And with the anger was the realisation that it was really over.

'You'll have to speak to him,' my daughter had said. 'You can't just leave the phone on answer machine.'

He didn't love me. I'd given up too much for him. And then, when thinking these things, I'd become inspired to start all over again. Excited, I'd think I could do it differently next time, if only he'd agree.

'You have to suffer more,' Annalyse had said. 'You have to suffer more before it's over.'

Across the road, a woman sits on a cardboard box near the mall. In front of her is a pack of brightly coloured tarot cards. She looks up when I approach, her silver hoop earrings and thick silver cross glittering in the light.

'How much does it cost?' I ask.

'Twenty-five dollars for both the cards and the palm reading. Twenty dollars just for the cards.'

'How much just for the palm reading and not the cards?'

'Twenty dollars.'

'I may as well have both.'

She stubs her cigarette out on the pavement. 'Why not?' she says. 'Be daring. Treat yourself.'

I sit down on a wooden crate in front of her.

'Shuffle the cards to put your own energy into them,' she instructs. 'Now cut them twice with your left hand.' She reaches across and strokes my hair. 'Beautiful hair,' she says. 'Choose a card, gorgeous woman.'

Digging deep into the pack, I choose a card and then turn it over. As she examines the card I watch her face closely.

'Are you in a rut?' she asks.

'Yes.'

'Everything will come together for you but you have to change,' she advises. 'But you need to leave the country first to get out of the rut.'

'Can't I just catch a train somewhere?'

She shakes her head, then studies the card again. 'Cut the cards and choose another one.'

I watch her face closely again as she frowns at the card.

'Your father was the strong one in the family,' she states.

'People used to say that my mother had my father flat on the ground with his shoulders pinned to the floor,' I say to the woman on the stool.

I see Father's face. I'd asked my half-sister what she remembered of his violent outbursts.

'Your father was very good to me,' Inez had snapped. Then she added, 'And don't you ever ask me about that again.'

The woman on the stool picks up my hands and uses a magnifying glass to inspect both sides of my little fingers. 'I come from a family of palm readers,' she says. 'I can see that you've had many past lives. You're an evolved soul. But you've experienced a lot of pain in your life and that little girl inside you is very hurt and vulnerable. You have to look after her.'

Seeing my sadness, she apologises. 'I have this effect on people,' she says. 'That's because I'm the Mother. A Taurus.' She stands up and holds out her arms. 'Here, let me give you a hug.'

'How can I look after myself better?'

'Use your intuition.'

'But how can I get in touch with it more?'

'Listen to it.'

But the voice is so faint, so weak, and so far away.

That morning in the gym at the retreat, the aerobics instructor said that if we want to make it harder we need to wave our arms around more. He turned the music up on the small black tape recorder on the floor. 'But whatever you do, do it with control,' he said. 'Make sure you've got great posture all the way through. Hold in those stomach muscles. Feet wide apart, toes out, abdominal tilt. Exhale down, shoulders down. A soppy number to start with. Lift and reach. Back and over. Reach and over. Other side. And again. Left. One more time. Feet out wide. Side to side. Left left. Keep going. Five, four, three, two. Left. Over. That's it. Back with four, three, two. Arms up and over. Push. Eight more. Eight, seven, six, five, four, three, two, one. Power walking around the room as fast as you can. Have a drink, do up your shoelaces. Now's the time to do it. The slower walkers on the inside, the fast walkers on the outside. That's it. One more lap. Go, team. It will bring your heart rate up, your heart rate down.'

'Time for some abdominal work. Roll yourselves down. Breathing out. Breathing in. Keep your back flat. Your tail on the ground. One more time. One, two, three and four.'

The exercise bikes, walkers and weight training equipment were reflected in the full-length mirror at the front of the room.

The trainer told us to get a mat from the side of the room and to lie on the floor for the relaxation session. 'There are pillows available too if you want them.'

There were about ten people in rows with their feet towards the mirror.

The personal trainer stood over us giving out the instructions. 'Try and keep your awareness on your body, where it is, how it feels. Have an awareness of any thoughts that come into your mind. Be aware of any emotions as you lie here.'

On the way out of the gym, we threw our used towels into a cane basket by the door then lined up for a drink at the filtered water cooler.

The woman with the white nails came up to me. 'You did that class with vigour,' she said.

The afternoon is closing over. I walk along the gentle curve of the street that follows the railway like a riverbank. Ragged storm clouds cross the sky, heavy with rain. They stain the mountains with black shadows. Pausing high above an amphitheatre of rock, I watch the sunlight fade. The great sandstone escarpment has turned from orange to deep purple and then faded into violet. Below me, the river moves between the ferns as darkness eases across the rocks. The wind lashes my hair and the dampness of it all works its way up from my socks.

Part Two

Charoses

Finely chopped nuts and apple, moistened with wine, represent the morsel of sweetness to lighten the burden of unhappy memory. – *Jewish Cookery* by Leah W. Leonard

Perhaps a lot of time must pass before one can really know or understand what took place. It's so difficult to show pain and suffering in words. I remember the fair-haired man I met at the poetry festival who'd said that when his son left home he had nothing to live for any more. 'I lost all desire to continue living,' the man had said. 'I'd wake in the morning and think, shit, I'm still alive.'

The telephone rings while I'm cleaning up my desk. I'm tidying up to make room for a new chapter to happen. I am a ghostwriter who tells other people's stories that I am commissioned to write. My days are spent in the library, walking through cemeteries, going through old letters and journals, or visiting old people's homes and, against great odds, getting words on the page. Since beginning this particular story, three years ago now, I have explored and examined tombstones, names, dates, epitaphs as I attempt to sift the truth from a quagmire of facts.

My desk is by the window in the bedroom and faces the east. This morning it's dull and overcast, although the light still penetrates through into the room and I have to close the curtain behind the computer in order to reduce the glare behind the screen. Under the desk is a cardboard box filled with notebooks, the bedside cupboards filled with more notebooks and reams of paper.

I have been throwing out old drafts of previous chapters to give some order to my workspace, which is covered with remnants, bits and pieces, research material, ideas on scraps of paper that are pinned to a clipboard by the side of the computer.

Also pinned up at eye level are pictures of men and women dancing in couples. In one, you can see the stretch of a woman's body up from the waist, the man behind her, his hands on her waist as she leans back and into him. Her dress flows down over the firm curves of her body and then flicks up on one side to reveal her thigh. Her arms are above her head, her face showing the ecstasy of the dance.

In another, a cutting from the newspaper, a professional tango couple are in the staged embrace of the dance, heads in line, noses touching, her gloves black, his suit dark, her thigh exposed as her leg is lifted and wrapped around the man's body.

I had worked my way through several piles of old papers and was almost through the remainder on the right of the printer when I'd come upon the photo of Mother as a young woman. This photo, kept in a plastic sleeve, is the only picture of Mother that I can bring myself to look at.

In the photo, Mother looks different to the bitter disappointed woman I'd known. She's young and carefree, long hair to the waist, shiny satin trousers. Mother and I look nothing alike. In fact we are, or rather were, nothing alike. Where Mother was tall, I am small; Mother a blonde, whereas I am a brunette.

I put the photo down and go to answer the phone. 'Hello,' I say. 'Sofia here.'

'Sofia. How are you? What are you doing?'

'Sorting through some stuff, cleaning up a bit. Hello, Inez.'

'What do you think about the weekend?' says Inez. 'Does it still suit you to come?'

'Yes. What about you?'

'I feel a bit nervous about it. I've hardly seen you over the last six months. We used to be close but not recently. We seemed to get on better when you'd come and stay.'

'That's why we've planned this weekend together,' I remind my half-sister. 'I'm still coming,' I say with reassurance in my voice.

I was four when my half-sister left home to get married. Recently, Inez said the tables have turned. It's my turn to take the lead. She's envious because I have a daughter and she, Inez, has only sons. She'd like to have a daughter, especially now. Now that she's older and not well and with a sick husband to look after.

'Let's make it for the day then,' I say, 'not overnight. I'll come for the day.'

'No. Let's leave it as it is,' Inez continues. 'I'm not the person I used to be, you know. You'll understand that, won't you?'

'Of course I understand,' I say, picturing Inez's sideways walk, the walking stick, and the whole damn situation. I close my eyes, see myself lying in bed at Inez's house, propped up in the double bed and Inez coming in to say goodnight in her nightgown, her long white hair pulled up tight with elastic on top of her girlish freckled face.

Mother too used to have a walking stick to help her move around her darkening world. She'd lift her stick and point it like a gun and say, 'If I had a gun, I'd shoot them all.'

'By the way, do you know where our grandmother's grave is?' I ask my half- sister. 'I know which cemetery but not where in the cemetery.'

'You mean Mamma? I know exactly where Mamma's grave is. I know where she is in the cemetery but I don't know the number, the plot number. You know Mamma was a mother to me. She was the one who was there to meet me when I'd come home for the holidays. Mother had to work of course.' This Inez says in a tone that suggests Mother had no choice and it must have been very hard for her and of course she understands why Mother wasn't there when she was growing up.

'Would you be interested in going there and showing me where the grave is?' I say. I never knew this grandmother, Mother's mother. I would like to have known her.

'I've never been back,' says Inez. 'I would quite like to go back there.'

'Well, let's plan an outing. The art gallery, lunch, whatever.'

'No. We'll stick to the original plan,' Inez says in a hard, determined voice. 'We'll get through it.'

'We'll get through it! I'm definitely not coming if that's the way you feel about it. Let's go out somewhere instead. What about visiting the cemetery? How would you feel about going there? Inez?'

A few birds flap past the window as I watch. I rub my finger across and then begin to draw a star of David on the glass as I wait. The sun struggles between the northward moving clouds. It bears down on the row after row of television aerials that rise up above the blocks of red brick units that line the sides of the gorge like an amphitheatre. The sun seems to transform the aerials into crucifixes that reach for the sky.

'Yes, I would like to go back and see Mamma's grave,' Inez says. 'I wouldn't be going as some sentimental thing, though.'

Time and again, I've rejected the idea of looking into my own family history. But thoughts of the relationship between my half-sister and me have persisted, and slowly, reluctantly, I am attempting to make sense of our connections, or rather, lack of connection.

If I now say that a dog barks on one side of the gully and another dog on the other side, birds twitter in the trees, that there is the agitated and dramatic sounds of Rachmaninov's No. 1 prelude in C Minor, that the sky is filled with clouds, that the sea and the horizon behind the tall strands of bamboo are hazy in the morning light – if I say this, then I mean that I'm trying to create an atmosphere in one way or another.

A large bird flies up out of the flame tree.

After hanging up, I throw the rest of the papers into the bin and walk down the two flights and go to the car in the last garage in the row under the block of units. I get in, turn on the ignition. A voice on the car radio says, 'The browning lawns of a water-restricted Sydney…' I look through the dust-covered back window and then reverse up the driveway; drive east.

The Pacific Ocean rocks slowly. I look at the people who hurry along the footpaths with shopping bags and notice the other cars clotted with dirt, their chassis spotted like a Dalmatian's coat. I'm trying to forget myself, to be interested in the world around me; in people, in things – the world. I feel despicable.

Mother had said she'd had enough of life. 'I may as well throw myself out the window,' she said.

I find the place, a small house on a corner next to a children's day care centre; park out the front and go inside. The dance studio is out the back. It's dim. Red curtains on the side windows, yellow curtains on the main door. Four grey plastic shiny chairs joined together at the end of the room provide a place to sit and change your shoes. Covering the whole long expanse of one long brick wall is a panelled mirror. Plastic vines hang between the panels. There's a print on one wall of a bull locking its horns into the red outstretched cape of a slim, curved-spine matador. Next to the print are Reg's teaching certificates and the awards and the photos of when he was younger dancing with women in flowing dresses and slicked-back hair.

Reg is starting up a lesson with Boris. Boris takes off his jumper and stands up tall in his shiny black patent leather dance shoes. The shoes seem to transform him from a man with a pot belly in dark trousers and a white shirt into a man who is light on his feet. A dancer. Reg throws his own knitted vest towards the music booth behind the row of plastic chairs. With a straightening of his back and the projection of his chest, Reg indicates to Boris that he is ready. Boris wipes his sweating palms down the side of his trousers.

When the music stops, Boris walks over to change his shoes. 'I'm Boris,' he says to me. 'Boris with a B. What's your name again?'

The music of a foxtrot starts up and Reg calls out, 'I'm ready.'

I get up and walk up to him.

With his body erect, he waits for me to position myself. 'Put your arms in position. Tighten your body before the man steps up to you.

Let him place his arm on your back before you put your hand on his shoulder. Lean out left.' He leads me backwards.

I stretch out long as he dances to the side, indicating from the angle of his body a feather step and then into a heel turn.

'Connect at the hip so you know what the man is going to do. Move your head back towards the wall as you turn. Stay down low. Only rise up when you turn to the front.'

We gather momentum as we move faster around the room.

'Stay heavy-footed on the balls of your feet. Drive, drive, then up, up when you walk outside me. Bend the knees and down into the floor for the down, down.'

Two figures reflected in the glass as we spin, run, spin, turn, run again in unison. Two figures all in black.

I can see the season is changing. It has many faces, this place where I live. The sand is white, the water clear and blue, with curling waves – although there is a dangerous rip. The beach has its own moods: from huge seas and giant surf, to the peace of a flat, calm alcove, and from a bright, blue ocean to steely-grey waves, with bitter southerly winds, the sun dim behind the clouds, a cool breeze across my bare feet and legs. On the radio a voice says, 'Rest is a musical term for a pause between flurries of notes. Without that tiny pause, the torrent of notes could be overwhelming.'

I hand Inez her walking stick as we wait to cross the road and then head towards the iron gates of the cemetery. The grave is so overgrown it's amazing that my sister recognises it. We peer at the faded white inscription on the brown marble plaque.

Inez says, 'You know how Grand Mamma died, don't you?'

'Yes.'

'She had a fall three weeks before she died. It must have caused a blood clot that went to her heart or to her brain. What do you call that?'

'What made her fall over?'

'Dead at fifty-two,' Inez answers, looking off into the distance. 'Some things are best left unsaid. You know she was alcoholic? You know that, don't you?'

I shake my head and say, 'I don't know anything. It all happened before I was born. I was told so many stories I never knew what to believe.'

'I can still picture Mamma coming out of the bottle shop down there at Rose Bay. I was sixteen. I can still see her walking out of that shop.' Inez wipes her cheek with a tissue. 'My eyes water in the wind,' she explains. 'The grave looks like no one cares.'

'We could clean it up. I'll do it. If you've got something to cut the grass with.'

'I could never do it.'

'I know. I'll do it.'

'I have got some secateurs, but the grass is so high. It would be hard work.'

'I could do it.'

'I'll ring the cemetery and see if they've got some service to clean up the grave. I'll pay for it. I'll pay the money to have it done.'

'I could do it.' I sigh.

'Leave it as it is,' Inez says decisively, concluding the conversation.

The thin, almost bare branches are stark against the brightness of the blue of the cloudless sky.

'You know how Mother met your father, don't you?' asks Inez.

'Every time, she told me something different. I asked many times.'

'Mother had a friend called Amy. Amy was Jewish. That's how they met. And you know the story of Amy?'

'She drove herself over the cliffs. With the married man.'

A helicopter, its blades spinning, its motor humming travels south through the sky. Then it's quiet again.

The pilgrimage to the grave is on my mind in the morning when I get up and open the sliding glass door. After breakfast, I ring Mother's sister, her much younger half-sister, to tell her I've been with Inez to see the grave. 'Do you know where it is?' I ask.

'Yes,' says my aunt. 'Diamond Bay. Near the road. I haven't been back. It was a terrible thing for me. To lose your mother at fourteen. My mother had a tough life. A daughter dead of cerebral palsy at six. And then my father left her because it was all too much for him – the cerebral palsy. A son dead in the war.'

'What do you remember of that time?'

'I remember the knock at the door and the person who brought the telegram. It must have been terrible for the mothers who had a son at war. Every knock at the door must have brought so much anxiety. She sent me down to the post office to pick up the telegram. She couldn't face it.'

'Do you remember much about your mother, my grandmother?'

'I remember everything,' she exclaims. 'How she looked. How she was. You know how she died?'

'Yes.'

'She was cooking dinner. Tripe, peas and potatoes. When Wally got home, she was dead on the floor. The dinner was still cooking. Her cigarette was still burning in the ashtray. It must have just happened.'

'What do you remember about her?'

'She was very beautiful, as your mother was. You have to admit that.'

'Yes, Mother was very beautiful.'

'I was the ugly one. My mother was very beautiful too. You've seen that photo of her?'

'Yes. What happened to the photo?'

'I would have liked it. Inez gave it away. Inez loved her so much, I thought she would like to keep the big picture in the frame.'

'I thought she gave it to you.'

'No, she gave it to my Karen. Karen doesn't want it. Inez was my mother's favourite, and I was your mother's favourite. Inez and I were like sisters. It's very painful to me that she won't have anything to do with me now. It must be a very deep-seated psychological thing.'

'I don't know. It all happened before I was born.'

'I'm thinking of trying to ring her again. She did write to me, you know.'

'I didn't know that.'

'I wrote her a long letter when she was in hospital. When she had the hip replacement.'

I saw the sun rise this morning, the light of the dawn at last. The sound of the waterfall after the rain, down in and through the gorge. A white butterfly soared across the long shafts of the bamboo. I love living within earshot of the waves, the soft ripples of white. A car sparkles in the morning light as it makes its way around the curve of the road near the edge of the cliffs – the cliffs that form a boundary with the sea. But it is the treacherous sea which is always most frightening. My cruellest dreams are flooded with water. The ocean seeping in, creeping up, the giant unexpected wave.

The world was wild as I'd jumped the waves, the sea a darker different kind of a blue, with huge motions of movement towards the shore as the waves broke loudly one behind the other.

'Sofia, Sofia,' J had called out as he moved up the escalator towards me.

I didn't hear him at first, my mind on other things. So there he was balancing a bicycle in one hand and a cappuccino in the other. He wore shorts and a T-shirt that showed off his muscular body.

'Wait for me at the bottom,' he'd called out, 'I'll come down.'

The passengers were continuing to pile out of the train. We'd kissed hello and I'd inhaled a stale lingering odour. I'd assumed it was from the exertion of riding his bike and dismissed it. My first big mistake.

Last night, I watched a storm. In the black night, black seas had broken in wild lines almost to the horizon. I'd cowered in my room with fear.

All I know is that I am driven by a desire to expose some facts and to find some meaning in the confusion. But I also have this overwhelming sense of resistance. Perhaps it is the day outside that is beckoning me to leave the seclusion of my office. Perhaps it's the boredom of going over it all again and again, until some new thing, some spark of something else, reveals itself from pure persistence of will.

In the early morning light, J had said he wanted to meet my children. 'If not now, then later,' he'd said. 'I want to be part of things.'

As a little girl, my bedroom window overlooked an oak tree. I would lie in bed and watch the movement of the leaves in the tree and the flights of the birds. I grew up in a big house, a kind of overgrown mansion filled with small rooms and odd corners.

There were twenty-one steps in that house. An old two-storey place on top of a hill, up a long driveway. The roof leaked when it rained. Mother put buckets under the drips. A pantry of biscuits. A wireless in the lounge room that we'd gather around. Then after their parties my brother and I would creep downstairs in the morning to eat soggy peanuts and leftover lollies smelling of cigars. Pansies. A front lawn to play on. A huge backyard where we kept our pets and had cracker night and I climbed the trees. We had a goat that ate the grass. My brother and I looked after people's pets in the holidays. We buried dead guinea pigs and rabbits that a dog had killed in the backyard. At night, I'd put out the empty milk bottles – carry them down the long driveway, then run back up or run down to the postbox at the end of the street with our dog, Skippy, then run up the hill to the house, then up the steep driveway, then run up the steps in the house two at a time. Twenty-one steps I counted every day in that place.

I asked my brother, the one I'd grown up with, if he remembered what kind of trees we had in the backyard of our old house.

'Suburban gums, I suppose,' he said.

'What kind of gums?'

'If you want to find out, go to the Botanic Gardens and have a look,' he said dismissively.

'Do you remember climbing those trees, playing in the trees?' I persisted.

'No, I don't. It's a long time ago. Over forty years. We move on.'

'Do you remember anything about the vegetation at all? I remember being outside in our backyard a lot, climbing the trees and going through our neighbours' backyards and through a block of flats to get to the next street up the hill. Do you remember that?'

'No. None of that.'

'What about the rabbits and guinea pigs we had?'

'Yes, I remember those.'

'And the roof leaking when it rained. Mother used to run around with buckets when it rained.'

'I don't remember that at all.'

'What about the pansies in the front garden?'

'I remember those. And the poppies. He had me working in the garden every weekend.'

'Did you? I don't remember that.'

'Yes, it was the tradition in those days. That was the male role, to look after the garden.'

'Let go of the past,' my sister said forcefully, with intention, just like my brother, before hanging up. 'Stop torturing yourself.'

I close my eyes: I am the little girl lying in bed, the covers tight, eyes turned toward a closed door, my dolls lined up on the window seat. Waiting for Mother. Struggling against sleep waiting for her to come and give me a kiss goodnight. Then there is the scent of perfume, the rattle of jewellery, the rustle of clothes. Beautiful, perfumed, her hair in waved fingers flat against her face. A peck on the cheek. Nothing, more.

There are certain ways I like to remember things about J, but I know it wasn't exactly like that. Well, it was, but there are other things too that I don't mention, that I'm too ashamed to say. Other things that happened that night and on other nights. But still, it could have all been over then, after that first night, without any harm being done.

'The two things you want to get control of when dancing are your body and your mind,' says the dance teacher at the tango workshop. 'You can help your body by breathing properly. Before you start, consciously take a couple of relaxing deep breaths. If you're tight, and you don't breathe, your tightness will get worse.'

In partners, we take turns to see if our partner's shoulders are going up and down, indicating shallow breathing.

'Proper breathing is with your diaphragm. Breathing into your lungs will leave you wanting air and tense. Breath in and exhale. Breathing from the belly rather than shallow breathing from the upper back. No rising of the shoulders. Keep breathing as you dance,' he says. 'Make sure your neck and shoulders, while your arms are strong in the frame, are relaxed. You're all dancers. You need to look like a dancer not only on the dance floor but when you walk down the street. Walk down the street like you would do normally. Now adjust your posture and your eye level and your breathing and walk back the other way. Walk with intention. Eyes level with where you are going, projected ahead. See how different it is. See if you can walk straight with a blindfold on by keeping your knees together.'

We take turns in groups walking in a straight line across the basketball stadium with our eyes covered by a black blindfold. Then in pairs, one with a blindfold leading, one without blindfold, following.

Sounds carried well in our old house, from room to room and up the stairs.

'She's only a child,' I'd heard Father shout downstairs.

I hung further over the banister but could not hear Mother's reply. A match was struck and I imagined Father leaning across to light Mother's cigarette and putting the spent match back in its box with those large thick hands of his.

'She'll be in high school next year,' said Mother and laughed her nasty laugh.

'What are you doing letting her buy a dress like that?' Father sighed.

Blood rushed to my head from leaning so far over the banister, but although I wanted to hear more, no more was said.

In my bedroom along the corridor, I could hear most things.

'You're making her grow up too quickly,' Father maintained, as sound flowed from one room to the next.

I was hanging over the banister at the end of an empty afternoon when Father and Mother entered the lounge room and Father said, 'Anika is nothing to me.'

I heard Mother's dismissive chuckle. There was a long silence in which I began to trace the curves and grooves of the curves at the top of the banister, but quietly. The scrolls of wood smelt of beeswax and dust and dirt gathered in the corners, but it was a fun place to be high up at the top of the staircase pretending to be invisible.

'Anika means nothing to me,' Father repeated.

I knew that our former housekeeper was married now and worked in Father's factory. The silence went on for so long I thought they must have gone out somewhere, but I could see Father's shiny shoes on the floral of the carpet. Something was making whinings and damp cries full of tears. He cried in the silence in a whimpering sobbing kind of a way.

The dance teacher walks along the line of us all standing in a row waiting for the next exercise. 'What do you like about tango?' he says. 'You have to tell me before you can have another turn.'

Susan volunteers, 'The closeness with a partner. The music. Being physically close to an attractive opposite-sex partner.'

Giggles and laughter from the group.

'You do it because you want to dance,' he says. 'You want to be engaged with the music and you need a partner. Keep reminding yourself that you love to dance, that by dancing in time with the music you will make a breakthrough to being the dancer you want to be.

Keep your frame up at all times when you move,' he says as he watches us dance in couples. 'Act a bit – move as if you were a great dancer already. Be one in your mind. Tango isn't about footwork, it's about all of you: body, mind and spirit. A good frame supports this.'

'I'm sorry I'm not as advanced as the rest of you,' apologises Alex, my partner for this exercise.

'That's fine,' I reassure him.

'I'm worried that I'm not good enough for you.'

'Don't worry about it. I just want to enjoy the music and to dance with a partner.'

'I don't know a lot of moves yet.'

'That's fine. I'm happy if a man does only three different sequences all night as long as he does them well.'

'What do you remember of me as a child?' I asked my much older half-brother, Jon.

'I don't have a lot of memories of you as a child – I left home on my sixteenth birthday and worked on a sheep station for two years, which was before you were born. Then I came home around Mother's Day that year and stayed till I was a few months past twenty-one. So I had three years with you. My memories are of you being a happy little girl but all the attention going to your brother. I remember you had a black and white cat and Mother telling you, "Get that cat out of here!"'

I'd spent a long time choosing what to wear before meeting my half-brother that day. I hadn't seen him for many years and wanted to create a good impression. He's seventeen years older than me, and I don't know him very well. He's my mother's son from her first marriage. The son she gave away.

'You look good,' he said by way of a greeting as he stepped off the ferry. He'd travelled from the airport to Circular Quay and then out to Watsons Bay. 'I'm pleased to see you've kept your weight down.'

'It's not easy.'

'A lot of discipline,' he agreed.

'I'm battling against heredity.'

We sat at a fish restaurant drinking champagne and watched the cabin cruisers rock gently in the sea.

'I went to see a psychiatrist a couple of years ago to see if there's anything wrong with me,' he said.

'How often did you go?'

'I went twice. He said there's nothing wrong with me.'

'What did he say?'

Jon wiped the corners of his mouth with the white linen serviette. 'He said that I need to speak up and say what I think more. To be more interesting with what I say. People like that sort of thing. He said I weigh my words very carefully before I say anything. And he said I'm very nervy. Well, I know that.'

Father had taken hold of my arm and led me downstairs to the dining room, opened the door with a kick of his shoe, his fingers digging into my flesh. 'Over there,' he gestured, and I stood by the mahogany table, inspected the details of the sails of the boat in the bottle on the mantelpiece. 'Sneaky,' he said. 'You're a sneaky sly little girl.' From behind me, he said in a husky but determined voice, 'Bend over.' I heard the sleeve of his shirt being pushed up his arm. 'Bend down.'

I closed my eyes and felt the heat rise to my cheeks as I hung there. He pushed my skirt up, bloomers down. When his hand came down it whipped against my skin. 'It doesn't hurt,' I told myself and heard a stifled scream from somewhere. Mother was far away in the kitchen.

'When you were about twelve,' my half-brother continued, 'Mother was telling you off in the kitchen. When I went to do something else, I said to her, "Mother, you're much too hard on Sofia. You'll lose her affection and goodwill if you keep her under pressure." Mother made some critical reply that I can't remember. I have two photos of you taken in about 1950. Mother was wearing a navy or red dress with big white spots and holding you. The other was of you standing on what I presume was a lounge chair. You had a gold bracelet on your left wrist. When I looked for photos for a family history journal, I received lots of your brother but only two of you, which was an accurate reflection of him being number one. In my journal, there's a photo of Mother aged thirteen or fourteen. She's on the plump side and certainly not attractive. I think her great beauty developed when she was about twenty. She was twenty-eight when she married your father. After your father's funeral, your brother showed me a photo of the two of them on their wedding day and commented, "Dad must have thought he had won the lottery.'"

There was J's invitation in the beer garden, my hesitation, his boldness, the noise of the car, my fear, the suburban streets at night, the ocean near my home at night, my garage and his computer in his backpack, my lounge room, his video presentation, the balcony, the wine, our conversation, his boldness.

When he asked me if he could come home with me to show me the video presentation in a quiet place, I said was it was fine where we were. I felt like a fearful woman, much older than he was. There's more that I don't like remembering.

He walked with such determined steps out of the beer garden.

I often was afraid to tell him what I wanted even when I had been with him much longer than a few hours. Of course, the fact that I agreed so readily must have shown how much I wanted to go off somewhere with him, despite my initial hesitation.

'And what about our grandmother?' I asked my half-brother, Jon.

'Mother's mother lived with Wally, her second husband, at 22 Dover Road, Rose Bay,' my half-brother said. 'Twenty-two was a block of four flats, two upstairs and two on ground level. They lived on the ground floor left-hand-side flat. It was very tiny. Just two bedrooms off a long hall, dining and kitchen at the end. Immediately inside the front door was a tiny lounge room with a built-in veranda. I can well understand why Mother couldn't have Inez and me there. The old girl

used to give me two shillings a week pocket money but I had to earn
it by walking down from Bellevue Hill every Wednesday after school.
The work involved scrubbing her bath and tiled floor with sandsoap –
a gritty smelly cleaning product of the day. The old girl was a real snob
despite her rather ordinary life. I gather that she was a hairdresser. She
smoked filter-tip cigarettes at a time that most people had never heard
of them. She liked to have biscuits, cheese and sherry late afternoons.
Her marriage to Wally was one of convenience but she refused to have
any contact with his family because they were "too common". Still, she
was kind to me in the two years I knew her.'

It starts to rain while the sky is still blue and the sun is out. The rain
turns into hail that covers the brown railing of the balcony with a fine
layer of white. The blue of the sky merges with grey clouds, the sea
muddied as it transforms itself into a blanket of grey. The hail plinks,
bounces, spits out against the railing as the thundering of the waterfall
gathers momentum. There is a flash of lightning towards the sliding
glass doors where I sit and watch.

One morning when we'd lain there together in bed, I'd wanted to say
to J, 'You're a very exciting lover.' But I'd hesitated to use the word
'lover' in case he thought that I had made a claim on him already.
Instead I'd said, 'I love the way that you touch me.'

'I love smoking,' he'd answered, looking toward his trousers flung
on the floor. 'I just love smoking.' He'd sighed.

'Mother married my father when she was aged fifteen years and seven
months,' my half-brother continued. 'She fell pregnant fourteen days
later. Inez was born the following year and I was conceived shortly after.
The marriage was over before Mother turned eighteen. When I came to
Sydney for your father's funeral, Mother hid me in the laundry. She didn't
want to have to explain to the cleaning lady who I was. Mother absolutely
destroyed any chance I had of gaining confidence. I realised immediately

there was a cover-up to avoid reading the will. There was never any chance that Mother would rank me equal to her other children. Mother said one thing that was correct: "You have been successful in material things but your personal life has been a disaster." But all I wanted in life was a backstop who wouldn't cause me pain. Mine has been an undeserved life of mental stress without the benefit of a mother's love.'

The fact that I must be mistaken about some of this doesn't bother me. There was the fact that I was slightly drunk and I didn't want to begin anything with him with me paying for the meal, and there was his enthusiasm to go somewhere quiet. The fact that he held my hand as we walked to my car. The way he offered to drive so I wouldn't lose my licence for driving over the limit. The roar of the car when he started it. The way he strapped himself into the driver's seat after first handing me my seat belt and waiting till I'd clicked myself in. The gentleness with which he did this. The cane of the lounge chairs. Then the awkwardness of the bright light by my bed. The sound of the waterfall as we stood on the balcony.

At dawn, he was asleep and I had to wake him up to make sure he left before my children arrived to cook me a Mother's Day breakfast. He said he wanted to meet them and to be part of the family, but it bothered me that he said it so soon.

'Needless to say, I would have far preferred to remain on good terms with all the family than be in the predicament I am today,' said Jon. 'The whole business regarding the will, Inez's deceit and the same secrecy as Mother's. Her extravagant gossip was often a gross stretch of fact. The claim that I had been expelled was outright vicious slander, although Inez would probably say Mother told her…which would not surprise me anyway. Mother achieved in death what she could not in life! Good health is the only thing that's important,' he said as we walked towards the ferry to say our goodbyes. 'Good health and a pocket full of money.'

It was then that I asked him the question that Inez had repeated many times, what about his own daughter?

'What was I to do with a two-year-old girl?' he said in his own defence. 'I couldn't cope with the upset of it all. I had access from two to five every Sunday. And if I was five minutes late, her mother wouldn't let me have her at all. So I gave up the access. I couldn't handle it.'

And then, as if speaking it for the first time he said, 'I did the same thing to my own daughter as Mother did to me.'

At the front gate, J had said, 'I'll call you in a day or two, okay?'

Then there was the click of the door. Through the glass I'd watched as he'd walked up the driveway. His determined step, his shoulders hunched with the computer in his backpack – which looked incongruous with his nice shirt and his tie and his new woollen jacket – his head forward from his neck as if needing to move faster than his body could carry him. I'd wondered if he had enough money for the bus and train but had decided it wasn't my problem so I wouldn't ask.

Even then, I'd thought, this is just a fling. It's only a fling.

I'm remembering being nine and brushing Mother's hair. Mother is sitting at a dressing table in a hotel room while I part it, roll it, secure it with bobby pins into a French roll. Mother reaches for a cigarette, lights it, settles down in front of the mirror. She blows the smoke out slowly. Her lips are perfectly formed, well defined, with two sharp bits above and a clean fine line curved below. And then her green eyes start on a sad reminiscence.

Two days later, he rang. I was very happy to hear his voice. He said that when he'd left my place he'd caught a bus to the station, bought a coffee and a croissant and then walked all the way home in the rain because he didn't have enough money for the train trip. 'I like living on the edge,' he explained. 'Thanks for a great night.'

'We're not meant to do that.'

'I know.'

When he'd arrived home that morning, he'd discovered that someone had broken into his unit and stolen his bicycle. He'd left the blinds up and he lived in a ground floor apartment.

He sounded distressed when he said, 'I hadn't meant to tell you all that. Can I take you out for dinner next Friday night? I'm sorry if I sound a bit drunk but I'm on to my fourth bottle of beer.'

He said he'd given $25 to a woman who came to his door asking for money and he thinks that she had a look around and decided to steal his bike.

And then there is Mother and me in front of the fire. This time, Mother is drying her hair while I watch. I see the graceful curve of Mother's neck as she leans forward towards the heat from the flickering fire. Mother's hands are shaking the hair out at its roots, separating the long blonde strands.

As I walk towards home, a black crow flaps through the dark tree limbs. There are stars and I can see darkness under the trees. A large woman in a black coat sways from side to side along the footpath outside the bottle shop. I recognise this woman, even from the back. I've heard her voice in the units after a drinking session. I'm about to move past quickly, expecting the woman to lurch and fall and I don't want to get involved.

But the woman buckles at the ankle and stumbles to the pavement in front of me. 'Will you help me? Will you help me get up?' the woman pleads.

I reach out my hand as she tries to stand up. Bracing my stomach, to strengthen the core of my body to take the large woman's weight, and bending at the knees, I allow her to use me to pull herself up.

'You're built like a sparrow,' Mother used to say when she'd hold onto my shoulder to steady herself.

We were sitting on the balcony drinking champagne one night and he said he'd like me to meet his mother. He said we'd like each other. He rang her long-distance from the phone in my bedroom.

'It's Doris,' he said handing the phone to me. 'Say hello to Doris.'

I told her that J had bought a bottle of champagne to celebrate the end of the research phase of a book I was working on.

'I hope he's behaving himself,' she said.

I asked her about her career as a journalist. She told me that J wanted to write too and that he had written some pieces. He hadn't told me about his desire to write.

Later, he asked me to read and critique a story he was working on that he planned to enter in a competition. I suggested a better place where he could start the story: the place where the character wakes up as a grown man alone in a bed in the room of a child. The child's mother is in the kitchen preparing breakfast for her children. It's a moving moment when the mother comes in to the bedroom and gently wakes him up and tells him she's taking the children to school. There are the sounds of the family preparing for the day and a man prostrate with despair sleeping in the bed of a child.

It's a beautiful winter's morning – cool, but without a cloud in the sky. All night I've tossed and turned, drifted in and out of consciousness but not really asleep. I watch the shifting light. A gentle breeze rustles the brown branches. Sun-dappled patterns of light and dark create patterns on the grass that I'd never noticed before. Bird songs resonate in the early morning stillness. I see a thick blue sky through the branches overhead and watch a bird's graceful path through the gorge. My life is actually much better since Mother died.

I look out through the diamond-patterned screen to the brown earth and the grass beyond and see the tree's lengthening shadow, the rocky patch under the bushes, the silver mesh of the fence. I listen for the voice of the wind, but hear my own loud sigh.

At the hospital, I'd said goodbye to the body. To the yellow wax-like face. 'I'm sorry,' I'd said. 'I did my best. I did the best that I could.'

I wind the car along the curves of the eastern coastline, the road that skirts the Pacific Ocean, up and around, past the long arc of glinting white sand and undulating cliff stretches. I park on the curve of the road that leads to the eastern perimeter of the graveyard that overlooks the ocean – this place where poets Henry Lawson and Dorothea Mackellar are buried. I get out of the car at that place where I come to watch the whales. All around me are people walking the path by the sea, people in shoestring tops, others carrying surfboards, their feet bare on this now overcast winter afternoon.

I walk up the hill along the sandy ground and into the Edwardian surrounds of the cemetery, along the aisles of geometrically placed graves.

At the door of a concrete vault, a man in boots and a fluorescent vest is talking about the placement of the thick concrete slabs in a family vault. 'You can fit six in here,' he says to his working mate. 'It's not full yet. There are three shelves. Two on each level.'

I continue past the Irish Martyrs Memorial and between the graves, glancing at the solid stone white marble monuments and inscription plaques – *The only pain she ever caused was when she left us* – and up through the wrought-iron gate that fronts the administrative centre.

I find the cemetery manager behind a desk, a stocky figure conservatively dressed in black trousers and neatly pressed shirt and tell him that I'd like to use his computer records to do a search of the cemetery.

'We can do it for you,' he says, 'for a fee of fourteen dollars. We're not online yet, like other places. Just tell me the name and the date of death, in case it's a common name. We'll do the search for you.'

I pay him the money and then go back outside to the garden memorial for cremated ashes with its inscription plaques, the plaques set on mellowed sandstone, granite and white marble – *Life is but a short time, Love is forever.*

The clouds are puffy and swollen where they surround patches of blue. At my feet, a white cockatoo, his yellow headdress displayed, bounces on a white flannel flower while a second cockatoo pecks at the grass. I look out again at the turquoise water that darkens to ultramarine blue out there, where the sea deepens.

As I walk back to the car, an offshore wind sweeps the white manes of spray from the crest of the waves as seagulls preen themselves on the grass.

I hear the wind howling between the graves.

*

'It's therapeutic what you're doing,' Dr Ross said. 'It's a good thing. Writing about abuse is very therapeutic. I get my war veterans to write it down, but not until after they've been seeing me for a year and I warn them that they'll feel all the same feelings again.'

I was conceived by accident. Mother was breastfeeding my brother at the time and thought she wouldn't fall pregnant, and anyway she thought Father wouldn't want children. She had two already from a previous marriage. This husband had left her. The first child she'd put in a convent to be educated by the nuns when the girl was three. The second she gave away when the boy was eleven months. All this boy remembers now is the smell of urine. The smell of urine in the pot under the bed in the foster home where he slept with an old woman. When the boy was eleven, his father heard that Mother was about to remarry, so the father rescued the boy and presented him back to Mother.

'Just call me Helen,' she said to her son by way of an introduction.

I read somewhere that each memory has its own light, smell, movement, words and colours. Its own sensations, emotions, feelings and thought. And that the most important thing of all about a memory is what came before and what came after that memory.

So it is that I became aware that the relationship between my half-sister and me is pivotal. I want to find out what the family situation

97

was when she left home at twenty-one to get married. I was only four. I need to find out these things before all those who remember have died.

We were sitting by the fire, my half-sister and me. I've always loved a fire and the warm glow when the flames catch and reflect on the walls, blinking and shining like stars but then dying out without warning.

'So how are you feeling?' I asked.

'Little things all the time,' she said. 'I think you misread me, you know.'

It was then that I asked a stupid question. A question to which I knew the answer, although no one had ever given it to me. But I thought today was a day to find out some things.

'I want to ask you about the period when you left home to get married,' I said. 'You've said before that you used to read me stories when I was a child.'

She tried to work out how old Mother was when she married, even though I tell her the age. Then she talked about my brother and the stories she used to read him and one story in particular that she read to him so many times, at his insistence, that she knew the story by heart. She repeated the story to me now. Every word of the story. I wanted to say to her, no, not him. What do you remember about me? Me and you? I asked her this question in various forms as the conversation continued but in each answer was contained my brother's name.

'At my wedding, you disappeared,' she says. 'You weren't even in the wedding photographs. Mother hustled you out. She disappeared you. I was very upset about that.'

Inez looked into the fire and said, 'You were my life. You and your brother. Before you were born, I took three months leave of absence from work – a month before you were born and two months after. The way people think about things is so different now. Mother was thirty-five. But to me she was very old and it was quite a strain on her.'

She turned towards me, her voice full of accusation. 'You've changed. I've shown you things. I showed you the letter I wrote to Mother. I showed you the letter after she died. You didn't seem very interested in it.'

'You showed me the letter but at the time you seemed disgusted with yourself for writing those things that you didn't mean, but you'd written the letter to try and please her. It was a grovelling letter.'

'She had a rotten life and I forgive her for all that. Grand Mamma kicked her out. She went to live at the Sandridges with me and some friends at Coogee. She was a window dresser and when the war came she was the manager at Woolworths and they sent her to Maitland, where she put me into boarding school.'

'Why did her mother kick her out when she had a small child?'

'I don't really know. Could have been anything.'

I watched the hypnotic flickering of the flames.

'Mother always had a housekeeper,' Inez continued. 'I was the one who played with you and read you stories and played with you at weekends. Mother and Father doted on you but they were a tough pair.'

'What was I like as a child?'

'A very quiet sensitive little girl. A bit in the background. Not outgoing like your brother. I loved you both to death. You were my life then. But you were off to school very soon after I left. Everything changes for children once they go to school. Once I got married, I was very happy. After that, for the next fifty years, my relationship with Mother was a telephone call once a week.'

She paused, narrowed her eyes, said, 'I just feel you torture yourself. Things are stressful for you. I loved you both. You're looking for something that wasn't there.'

It's a beautiful spring morning. An almost cloudless sky. The scum of milk across my teeth, my back pushed against the cushions, bare legs and feet warmed by the early morning sun. The sound of water over rocks and through the trees and bushes, the crash of the waves down on the beach. Swirls of white move north-east towards the horizon.

A slight breeze stirs the leaves of the flame tree. A few red flowers are partly hidden in the shrubs. A plane overhead. Birds call to each other in the trees. No sounds of renovations today.

Sometimes the sheer isolation of what I am doing causes me to doubt at times that I even exist.

A voice on the radio says, 'We're up to a very warm day here in Sydney. And the bushfire season is already upon us.'

I remember once – it must have been early summer – when I saw Mother sitting there at the kitchen table in her apron. She sat very still, gazing towards the window, her hands palm down on the table, her elbows tight by her side. She was leaning back slightly, her chin pressed in towards her neck in an unnatural way. I walked up to her. She gave me such a sad look I almost burst into tears. But instead I stroked her hand gently. She closed her eyes as I did it. I felt very close to her at that moment.

She opened her eyes. 'Just look at you in those slacks. Wear a top that covers your bottom if you're going to insist on wearing trousers.' Then she put her arms out to me and smiled and kissed me.

I was overcome with joy. Just as suddenly, she started to weep and said something about how she was such a witch at times. All I could do was stand there with my arms around her.

'What a fool I am,' was what she said, freeing herself and drying her eyes. Then she got up and left me there not knowing what to do.

We'd finished the tea, moved into J's bedroom. The room was next to a driveway and looked out through slatted blinds to the brick wall of the block of units next door. A double bed with an iron bedhead, the carpet covered with clothes and papers.

I looked around, then said, 'Nice bed.'

'Sorry about the mess,' he apologised.

I shrugged.

He looked wistfully at the bed. 'It's the only thing in this unit that's mine. It's the only thing I've taken with me every time that I've moved.'

We got into bed. He rolled towards me and kissed me on the mouth. Then he got on top and moved rhythmically. His eyes were closed. When he came, he made a long satisfied sound. It took him a long time. Then he rolled off.

He turned towards me, his eyes still closed, wrapped his arms around me, a leg across my body. I felt the weight of him, wondered when it would be okay to move. I wanted to go home. I waited until his breathing lengthened and deepened then pulled the doona up and over his shoulders before sitting up carefully.

'You're not going, are you?' he said, his voice thick with sleep.

'I'm exhausted. I need to go home.'

'Please don't go.'

'I'm not used to sleeping with someone. Well, not since the divorce.'

'Not used to sex?'

'No. Not used to spending the night.'

'Please don't go.'

I bent down and gently stroked his forehead. 'I'm sorry.'

'Please,' he pleaded.

I put my arms around him, pressed his head against my chest, kissed his hair.

'Please stay,' he repeated. He was begging now.

I stroked his hair again then got up and reached for my clothes.

I can still remember it. What I said and him lying there, pleading with me. It seemed that I was always falling into some trap, some situation where I should have seen it for what it was and that it would never develop the way that I wished for. Lame ducks. I kept unconsciously betraying myself. It had been the same with Mother. If only I could have tried harder.

The sky is dense with cloud. One cloud piled on top of the other. The sway of the bamboo in the wind, the same wind that brushes across my toes. Lilac flowers among the branches. The smell of approaching rain.

My stomach knots and sinks with the anxiety of it all. I want to abandon ship. Although I'm sure it's not unusual to be filled with fear and dread and self-loathing when engaged in a struggle – to feel a terrible despondency. Piles and boxes of paper everywhere.

There is a park that is a cone-shaped peak of an ancient sand hill rising to the heights west of Bondi Bay, topped by magnificent fig trees and one majestic Norfolk Pine. This tree used to be a landmark.

Victor lives here, beside this park. He is the brother of a friend of mine.

I ring the doorbell and wait for Victor to let me in. I imagine him on the other side of the door. He stands up and listens. Was that the front doorbell? He runs his hands down the apron before closing the dishwasher, turns the oven on and walks towards the door. He opens it. A tall man, with a full head of thick black hair, whispers of grey. His navy blue apron covers the bulges of his body. He lives here with his two grown-up sons and is learning to keep house for them – although twice a week, when the house is open for inspection, his cleaning lady comes in.

I kiss him on the cheek before following him into the kitchen. A long parquet-floored corridor leads to the bedrooms, the formal lounge room and dining area and to a large informal entertaining space that overlooks the harbour. In the kitchen, I sit on a round stool and watch as he cooks a meal for the two of us.

He talks about some article he's read that says the modern woman doesn't want to live with a man, but just wants to see the man two or three nights a week. 'The man would go home in the mornings,' he says wistfully.

'In the morning, or before the morning?'

'Whatever,' he says dismissively with a flick of his hand, not understanding the significance of the timing of the exit of the man.

So to clarify this point I say, 'The man goes home if he's got a car and can drive himself home. Otherwise you have to get up and drive him home or to the station.'

He stops at the microwave, looks puzzled.

'I had a bit of a slip-up last week,' I say with a note of apology in my voice.

'You're going to have to lift your game,' he jokes. Then, with a downward inflection in his voice says, 'I should be so lucky.'

This morning when the naturopath looked into my irises, I told her that I am having a lot of neck and shoulder pain on the right side, probably caused by the posture of ballroom dancing and Argentine tango.

'Ballroom dancing uses only one side of the body,' the naturopath said. 'Playing the harp uses both sides of the body. Or swimming. Swimming would be perfect. What star sign are you?'

I told her that I'm a Pisces, that I love submerging myself in the sea, but I'm not much of a swimmer. She said a couple of style correction lessons might be all that I need.

I was not the same with J as I was with other people. The only time I felt shy with him was when he read the poems I had written. Sometimes he liked them, at other times he seemed shocked and wanted to know if what I had written was something I had experienced myself. I didn't answer him directly. Another time, he said that one of the poems would fit in well in an anthology of lesbian poets. I told him that I didn't think I would let him read the things I had written. He also exhausted me. I had to leave him just to rest from it.

The sea looks different every day. Today it's a mid-grey tone, its surface moving in a gentle tugging motion as a container ship moves south along the horizon. A moist breeze brushes my cheek as the waves make a gentle hushing noise as they curl into the sand of the beach. I watch the colour creep slowly into the clouds. A flock of lorikeets balances on the bare branches in front of me. The radio says, 'It's a pretty chilly day, this wintry month of August.'

Last night I dreamt that I had a deformed right breast. The breast had two nipples, like Siamese twins, but inside the breast was a very hard lump, like a rock. I'd tried to move the rock with my hand, to try and dissipate the lump. It was weighing the right breast down, but it wouldn't dissolve. It stayed solid, firm and immovable.

I said that my sister and I were sitting by the fire, but in fact it was over the telephone that I'd asked her the questions.

She said she remembered nothing of the nine years she spent in the convent from the ages of three to twelve. 'My nine years in boarding school in Maitland are a total blank,' she'd said. 'It was only when I got double pneumonia that I got to go home. I loved you both,' she repeated, referring to my brother and me. 'But then I got married and had my own children. You know how it is when you have a baby? You think you'll never love anyone as much as that first baby, but you do. You have another one and you love them just the same. You must know that from having your own children?'

Yes, I knew what she meant

'Are you still seeing the doctor?' she asked.

'I hadn't seen him for a few months but I've decided to go back.'

'I'm very disappointed to hear that.'

'Don't you understand?' I was shouting and crying at the same time. 'Don't you understand? I need to talk about these things. I need to talk.'

That's when she'd said the bit about me looking for things that weren't there. 'If you need a listener, I'm here for you always,' she said. 'I've got plenty of time to listen to you. Just ring up and say, "I'm feeling low." I'll listen to you.' She told me to live for today, that the secret to life is being happy with what you're doing right now.

I said something or other that was meant to sound like I was grateful for what she'd told me.

I have often thought about, but never attempted, suicide.

I had forced myself to look into the dark void that contained images of Mother. It's true, that in some respects I'd seen that Mother too was a victim. I could have ended it there. I'd come to see that Mother was a victim and that she'd done the best that she was able to do. Some compassion and understanding then on my part. I could say that. But it's not true. It's not the way I felt at all.

'Tell me again what you said before,' I say to Dr Ross. 'Remind me what you said.'

'These people cost the health system a lot of money,' he says. 'They wreck havoc with the people around them, especially their families. Serious personality issues. Gross, appalling dysfunction.'

'I don't have to forgive her, do I?'

'You were dealt a lousy hand,' he says in that supportive way of his.

'So it wasn't my fault?'

He recaps his pen, closes his writing pad, walks to the door.

At dusk, the clouds finally open up to reveal shapeless patches of blue. Birds, a plane, the breeze through the trees and into my office.

So there it is then. No huge revelations.

A voice on the radio says, 'Australia has lost the men's two-hundred-metre freestyle relay swim for the first time in seven years.'

Easy does it, I say to myself. Just small steps. Small doable actions.

I turn the radio off. I want to hear myself think. Birds, a dog, the distant ocean, although I'm never really sure it is the ocean. Maybe it's the wind up the gully, or other sounds that the wind makes. A garage door opens, then the birds again, distant hammering, perhaps the waves again.

'Just one envelope off the pile at a time,' the doctor had said. 'Just select one envelope off the pile at a time. Write the cheque, address the envelope, add the stamp, reach for the next envelope.'

It is still spring. The moon is bright round and full up there to the north-east about halfway up; the first star, over there near the moon. I marvel at how this light in the evening sky creates a new universe out of nothing.

The day is softening into night, my desk in shadow as the sun moves behind the building. Birds hover in the trees as the wind blows across the surface of the sea. It's hard to know which way to go. Every day I fear that I can't do it. So I'm watching as it gets dark.

Tonight I'm thinking about the saddest bits. Thinking, for example, that the night was alight with thunder. Lightening cracked the sky. Just a flash and then darkness again.

That I loved him, and sometimes he loved me too.

I'll begin with the birds. Three birds flying in perfect but constantly changing alignment. So often there are three. And then a lone bird darts across the sky in the opposite direction.

On the radio a voice says, 'We need to know the history, the history of the before, and then to know how the person chose to continue living, what baggage they chose to bring with them, to incorporate the memory into themselves or to leave it behind.'

A door bangs shut behind me; footsteps sound on the concrete driveway leading from the back door just a second or two after the door banged. The flame tree throws a shadow on the cane chairs on the balcony. I stop working, put my hands and then my arms around my body and think of the feel of his skin.

How appealing, how irresistible that prospect of intimacy is, with the very person who can never give it.

After a day in which I have evoked J again, all the pain and disappointment and wanting him all over again came back. I try to guess where he might be and what he might be doing but cannot imagine it. His absence is still as heavy as the wave about to break above me, a wave that has appeared suddenly, and then it curls over me forcing me down to the bottom of the sea, where I'm helpless in the power and pull of its rip.

Last night, I dreamt about a man with a hook for an arm. I didn't realise at first that the man had a disability because he'd kept it hidden behind the counter. On the spur of the moment, I told the man I was going to see a free film as part of the film festival and asked if he would like to come with me. To my surprise, he closed up the shop, put on a freshly laundered shirt and said he'd come. That's when I saw the hook arm. As the evening progressed, I was surprised by how very quick and skilful he was in the use of it. He hooked me a chair and one for himself when we found the small cinema where the film was shown. He seemed interested in me but I wondered how I would cope with his disability.

Sitting at my desk trying to work, I saw the line of the horizon from a different angle as the sun beat down, heating up something outside so that its taint floated in on a breeze. It was the dank scent of the earth after rain, entering through the open door. It reminded me of the smell of his hair in the mornings and it came between me and my work. I wondered why all of this has to go on for so long.

Although it's a dark night, there is a small crescent-shaped moon over the sea. I've decided to take a walk to the house where I lived as a child. I put on a cardigan and step out into the night.

The house itself is no longer there. It has been torn down and a block of units stands in its place. As I walk down the steps towards the beach and mount the hill, waves loom in the fading light; streaks of white against the dark sea. Above me, clouds gather against a starless sky. I walk up the steps then stand at the lookout as the sea rolls in.

When I was growing up, this suburb was full of large houses and blocks of art deco units. Some of the houses were very grand and others fallen into disrepair like ours. Mother was ashamed of our house. It was basically a mass of rooms surrounded on three sides by wide verandas and wooden painted rails.

Walking along my old street and its rows of gums and mix of glass and chrome home units and white-painted mansions, I see the stairs that connect this street to Birriga Road. Those stairs that I walked up every day to catch the bus to school until Mother decided it was important that she drive me to school before she went to work. 'What will the neighbours think with you talking to boys at the bus stop?'

And there's the house where the boy with diabetes used to live. The boy who used to double me on his bicycle. I can still feel the imprint of his ribs under my hands. 'It's not ladylike for a girl to ride a bike,' Mother said. This boy's house had seemed a long walk from mine but now it seems just a short distance as I walk up our old driveway.

Sixty apartments share our old address. Forty units across the backyard and twenty on the driveway. The trees I used to climb in the backyard are all gone. No wild foliage, just bricks, concrete and cement, although one scrawny hibiscus droops over garage number twelve. A couple of branchless tree trunks wedge between the units and the fence of the block next door. Nowhere for the trees to branch out. No sunlight. Suffocating. Vines strangling trunks. Trees choking to death. I feel a thudding in my chest.

Drowning again and again. A recurring dream. And then I would wake and lie there waiting for the sound of the birds and the light of the dawn. I'd count slowly: one, two, three on the in-breath, one, two, three on the out-breath until I noticed the waves lapping up and into my bedroom again.

It was already too late when I was eight. I grew old at eight. It came on very suddenly. I saw the blood spreading over my grey bloomers. As the year lightened and turned hot, it got worse.

'Don't tell anyone,' whispered Mother. 'Especially your brother.'

January was too bright so I stayed in bed in the darkened bedroom.

I was ashamed of how I'd changed. I wasn't prepared for it. I leant against the pillow in disgust. I lost the desire to move. But as dusk came one evening in February, there was the gentle sound of the wind through the leaves.

I see my former self. The small child with hair pulled severely back at the sides of her large forehead, revealing an open face that seems always to be frowning. I can bring to mind a tall gawky adolescent with pimply skin with her arms crossed over her chest. She wears dark wool skirts in the winter with long shapeless jumpers over the top, perhaps a long pendant, or cotton print dresses in the summer with a cardigan. Her hands would clasp and unclasp in front of her. Ridiculous. Her hair looked ridiculous. The hair must have been cut into a fringe but instead it bounced up into one tight little ridiculous ball in the middle of her forehead.

So I was eight and three-quarters. Mother made me wear dresses with pleats and frills. I wore them with loathing. They made me look fat and childish, gathered at the waist with a Peter Pan collar.

That day my hair was in bunches hanging down in the front, not cut short at the back as usual, but long enough for me to put an elastic band at each side. To my own hair I had added the hair of our housekeeper. I wore her hair attached to my own. I was using make-up already. A crème pancake base that Mother had given me. 'Cover up those hideous freckles.' I don't know where I got the pink lipstick and the clear nail polish. Perhaps I stole them. I was wearing a little 4711 eau de Cologne.

The early morning light shines through the thick curtains, the mysterious light when it's raining but the sun is still shining through the clouds, the gentle glow from a full moon; the exhausting and suffocating heat of Sydney's humid summer days and nights. A solitary bird against a bright blue sky when all the shadows of a long night have faded. It's seven forty-five. I have overslept. There is no sound in the building. No footsteps, no cars reversing. I guess that everyone has gone to work.

On the radio, 'Just a couple of drops of rain during the night here and there.'

Mother was reclining in bed. Her eyes were closed and her hands crossed against her chest. Her mouth was open. Now and then she'd catch her breath as if gulping the air. At that moment, she appeared to be asleep.

Beside her, I pulled the dead bits off the flowers. I put the vase into place on the shelf above the bed and stared at a Picasso print of a woman's body sectioned into geometric pieces. I smiled at its startling arrangement of shapes. I reached for another vase and began my pruning.

Mother leaned towards me and, in a rush of tenderness, unusual in her, tried to hug me. I recoiled, unable to check the repugnance I felt for the touch of her.

My half-sister entered the room quietly.

I got up at once, throwing the bruised and browning petals into the wire basket by the door. I went over to the bed, and looked at Mother, who kept her eyes closed. 'She's resting,' I said.

My sister went over and turned off the bedside light until there was only the weak light from the window. She sat down so she could see Mother. She stroked Mother's forehead; leaned down over the face, used her fingers to exert pressure on the skin between Mother's eyes, pulled the skin across her forehead, pressed gently into the sides of her face.

Mother opened her eyes. 'You smell of garlic. I can smell it on your breath.' But then she let herself sink again. 'You're very good to me,' she whispered. 'I don't deserve all the things that you do for me.'

Inez continued to massage her head and face until Mother fell asleep.

Inez said, 'I think about Mother nearly every day. When Mother spoke to me in her clipped determined way, I often didn't understand what she wanted from me. I tried so hard, but of course I never managed to please her. Then she'd show her impatience. She was always impatient. With all of us. She'd had a hard life and I forgive her. I loved her because she was so – I don't know what to say, exactly – because she was always such an overpowering presence. But she could be so cold. I would come to her wanting some affection, some understanding even, she'd turn away from me and be so cruel or she was just too busy to even listen to me. Yet I felt for her, I understood, and now that I'm older I forgive her totally. If only I could see her again and tell her I wish now that I had tried harder and that if I had, things might have been different.'

'Your sister has decided to smooth the surfaces and to remember her mother as a saint,' Dr Ross concludes. 'Her mother had a hard life and now she's turned her into a saint.'

I'm imagining walking into the old house. Across a big enclosed veranda and in through the front door. A coat cupboard to the right, along another corridor to the maid's room and bathroom, painted a light green, then out to the back porch and the lock-up garage. To the left of the maid's room is the large kitchen with a table in the middle of the room and a pantry to the side. Behind the kitchen is the laundry, the room where I'd do the ironing.

Mother is at the table with Father in the dining room, with its mahogany furniture and red and gold flocked wallpaper. It's already dark and the thick lined curtains are closed. White linen tablecloth and solid silver glitter under the lights of the chandelier.

Husband and wife are dressed formally. Perhaps they've been to synagogue, or else they've been to the Chevra Kaddisha to pray for a dead relative, or they may have been to an afternoon tea at a friend's house.

Father is two years younger; his face jowled, his mouth relaxed, his eyes small and piercing; his smile is kindly but wary. His hands shake slightly. His hands are broad, with thick blunt fingers, and are mottled with pigmentation spots. The short moustache and the grey hair are neatly trimmed.

Husband and wife eat in silence. The silence is full of contempt – a shared contempt – or is the contempt more on one side than the other?

She wears white gold wedding rings that are simple in design, and two diamond rings. And around her neck is a necklace of marquisette with drop earrings to match. He has given her many presents of jewellery over the years.

He turns to Mother and tells her he's going to adjourn to the lounge room with the newspapers, is she going to join him?

She shakes her head. He shrugs at this, confirming, let's see who will break first. Who will be weakest in this mutual destruction of each other.

'What are you laughing at?' he says.

'Nothing. I'm not laughing.'

'Will we listen to a record in the lounge or will we go upstairs to bed?'

'I don't want to hear any records, thanks.'

She knocks the sugar bowl over as she reaches for the teapot. The fine bone china dish breaks into pieces and the brown granules spread over the white cloth. She glances at him in barely disguised fear, but he keeps on stirring his tea, looking straight ahead.

He finishes his tea, wipes his moustache with meticulous care then throws the creased napkin onto the table and stands up. 'It's getting late. See you up there.'

To the right of the top of the staircase is their bedroom. I imagine Mother sitting down at the dressing table and taking the pins out of her hair. It falls to her shoulders, the heavy weight of it released. She puts on her nightgown and then stands in the middle of the room.

'It's a man's world,' she says in an absent-minded, dispassionate voice.

Father enters the bedroom, walks towards her. He is wearing a navy blue satin dressing gown and is holding a book in his hand, his glasses pushed up high on his forehead. She walks past him, pulls back the sheet. The sheet is spotted with blood. He sees the blood. She smiles to herself.

The sounds and smells of the end of the day. The sky at twilight a deeper darker softer shade of blue grey. The clouds still puffy but stagnant. Faint hush of the sea. Traffic noises in the distance. A brief hammering. The horizon hazy, the sea no longer blue but a soft grey. The movement of the waves towards the south in lines of darker grey. Thudding music from the house in front but then it stops. The rumble of a plane overhead as it nears and then recedes. Moves closer and then moves away. Kitchen sounds from the unit next door. Another plane rumbles in the distance.

The heat is leaving the day although the leaves and branches of the trees are not moving. Then a breeze picks up. A dog barks; the cicadas start up. Street lights, headlights. The sea darkens and the thudding party starts up again in the house in front.

It's enough for me now just to think of J's face with that peculiar, stricken look. Was it only later that as I searched for the memory of his face and looked at it and then his whole body, so often motionless and turned in on itself that I either took his face out of my memory or returned it to when I stood looking at him still asleep in the bed?

If he's living around here, he may be beginning a day's work just now, since he never was one for any early start, or he may be sleeping with the doona over his head, unable to face another day. He may be listening to the sounds of the people around him preparing for work. Or he could be with that woman with the three children. Or he could just as well be living out west again.

Mother thought that God was cruel and hard. She told me so many times. But I assume that in her prayers she still turned to Christ. Originally a

Catholic, she'd converted to Judaism when she married my father. I'm imagining her long honey hair is rolled in a bun, her fine cheekbones high and chiselled, but her mouth held in an ungenerous curve.

Her eyes were red with lack of sleep. She had been lying for several hours wandering whether to get up or not. *It's better to get up, straighten out the body, turn on the bedside light, try and read.*

She got up and stood for a long time by the hospital window; there was moisture on the pebbles of the veranda outside. Everything out there in the garden was blurred and hazy.

Thank you, dear, Lord for giving me daughters. I needn't worry so much about what will happen when I go home... Sometimes I think I've had enough of this world. How am I to cope? Then I let myself sink and there's only one solution.

She turned off the bedside light then heard footsteps in the corridor. A nurse came in and took her pulse and her temperature, made notes on the clipboard before replacing it at the end of the bed. Or that is how I imagined it.

Outside the window, a bird clutches a branch. Leaves surround and envelop him as the wind moves through the leaves. He trills a contralto then darts off towards the sky, swift as an arrow. The wind heaves the branches and scatters the leaves as another bird with a flurry of wings and a nod of his head darts off.

'You should write about sex,' Mother had said in her bitter, accusing tone. 'You know all about that. That's something you could write about.'

I must have been five when I came running in with a painting to show Mother, the picture of the birds in front of the clouds, the red sun to the left with its rays of sunlight. 'I've got a present for you,' I said. 'Close your eyes.' I put the painting in her hands. 'Open your eyes.'

She looked at it.

I pointed at the birds. 'One bird, two birds, three, four, five, six black birds,' I said proudly.

'It's all right,' she said in her horrible dismissive voice. 'You don't have to count them all.'

I showed her the swirls of blue. 'And this is me with my feet in the water,' I said. 'And this is you standing behind me watching. And this is the purple woolly rug that we had on the picnic. This is you and this is me.'

I began telling the story of J with the end, with me using the last tea bag from the box. But of course the story didn't end there. This may be the last time that I make the effort of remembering J. The last time that I let him make me suffer. It's the forgetting that takes so long.

Memories of Mother have almost faded altogether. I don't remember if I ever loved her. In my mind, I no longer have the feel of her skin, nor in my ears the sound of her voice. I can't remember the exact colour of her eyes, except sometimes I can see them all misty and watery with some secret. Her weeping I can't hear any more – neither her weeping nor her laughter. It's over with her, I don't recall the details.

That night in June, a strong wind had blown through the leaves. So strong it blew small branches off the trees and on to the car. Dirt blew along the road. Thunder, louder this time. A car alarm sounded for three beats and then it was silent again. Then more thunder. A plane flew into the grey, its lights flickering as the horizon blurred and became fuzzy and the sea turned into deep dark grey. People had flocked to the beach during the thirty-four degrees but now they hurried home as lightning split the sky. Thunder louder, although strangely the sky was still visible above the ocean and beneath grey clouds, still lit by the setting sun even as it began to rain.

I'd taken off my nightie and sunk into the hot salt and oil, stretched out as the phone continued to ring. I lay there and listened. He hung up without leaving a message. I'd felt the grief rising up from my stomach.

A bird plummets to the earth and J is no longer here. I sometimes find it hard to bear. After all this time, I'm talking about it to be free of it all, although I know I never can be. Over there to the east is the same sky reflected in the same water. But I am not the same, not the same as I was then, and not the same after telling it.

Outside, down in the gully, kookaburras are singing. The light of the dawn through the curtains casts long shafts across the carpet. A gentle breeze through the bamboo. A white sail against low hanging cloud. I watch the progress of the boat across the horizon.

Part Three

1

Painstaking Progress

I'm in my room, half office, half bedroom. Not too large and not too small. The windows of the room face east and look out towards the ocean across the expanse of a green gully.

I'm sitting on my bed with pillows behind my back. The windows are open. It is Saturday morning. On the bedside table is a mug of tea and a photograph of my daughter on her wedding day.

The wind begins to stir the big trees outside and the morning haze is beginning to move and for a short moment the sun lightens the carpet and heavy dark wood furniture. The shadows of the curtains' curves darken the floor, almost invisible to me on the bed. The morning sun lightens the CD player, the alarm clock, the piles of books stacked on the revolving Victorian bookcase.

I look out at the water and at the triangle of beach. Sometimes it seems that nothing much changes out there, although on some days the waves break close to shore and at other times further out to sea. I can see it all from the bed, even at night time. The bed faces the beach and the ocean, and so does the desk. The room is like standing at the rail of a ship.

On the radio, 'Waves, to me, are a reason to live,' says the surfer. 'When you see the roar, the jaws, there's nothing that touches it on the face of the earth.'

In June, the twilight begins in the afternoon. The days close in on me, here in this room. The infinite possibilities in the sky and the sea and the possibility of nothing.

Still no rain.

During a cool night, the drought continuing, my nightmare is that I am stuck in a narrow laneway unable to turn back. I get out of the car to attempt to turn it with my bare hands. But when I turn round to pick the car up, it has disappeared. I took my eyes off it for one second and it disappeared. Gone in the second that I lost sight of it. The desperation descends on me.

I snap on the bedside light just before the dawn. Dawn through the gorge. Leaves slight in a breeze, the dark green of the date palms. This shy light is flashing a start to the day. In fifteen minutes, the gorge will come alight in all its subtleties, water flowing across rocks, white butterflies.

The driest May in over seventy years.

I was relieved when my new friend Tom left the room, so probably it's already ending. But I'm not sure. I pay close attention to the surroundings, to the people in tracksuits trudging through the sand on the beach, the noise of the traffic up the hill, the static that immerses the room.

He glances at me. At first he looks at me as though he expects me to speak, but I don't. So he says, Don't worry, we'll get through it. Then is silent.

I don't answer. I could reassure him, could say, Yes, that's right, it's a small thing, we'll get through it. I say nothing.

He'd said he hates being lonely. I said, I'm lonely, horribly lonely. He said, It's a horrible thing, loneliness.

Every day, my father experienced a deep melancholy about living. Sometimes it lasted, sometimes it would vanish with the night. I had a father so desperate with sadness that sometimes even life's surprises, those very special moments, couldn't make him forget it. It happened every day. It would come on very suddenly. At a given moment every day, the melancholy would make its appearance. And after that would follow the struggle to go on, to sleep, to do anything, or sometimes the anger, just the anger, and then the despair.

In the dream, I was sleeping in a motel. I saw Father, like a floppy puppet with a wooden head, sitting on the far side of a room. He had strings attached to his hollow body and was unable to speak. The intensity of my grief woke me. I sat up on the big bed and I was by a lake, the sounds of a party under the window. Headlights bounced off the bridge and into the room through the thick curtains of the motel room. A small fridge clicked in the corner. I had been crying and the bones in my chest and in my cheeks were collapsed. I kicked the sheet off, curled around a pillow and stayed like that for the rest of the night. I became aware again of the powerful wind over on the beach and the waves curling and breaking and disappearing into the cold sand all the way along the central coast.

Today, the sea is twice the depth of blue as the blue of the sky. The clouds change shape as I watch, drifting south, melting and thinning. At the end of the day, their edges will be circled with pink.

When Tom came to visit the first time, I was pleased he arrived in time to see the brief pink light on the gully. From the balcony where we ate, we looked out over the round bowl of the gorge, ringed with blocks of apartments and filled with cypress and palm trees. Branches like whips; leaves every shade of green you can imagine. Rosellas and cockatoos. We heard the flock of kookaburras at dawn.

There's the click of the front door. He walks in. His hair is tumbled, his lips stained with sunburn; I tell him he looks like he's had a good time down at the beach and what a good arrangement it's turning out to be.

He has something to tell me. Would I like a cup of tea first? He's going in to the kitchen to make one for himself.

No, no thanks. I've had one already. But help yourself and then tell me what happened.

He opens the door out on to the balcony, hangs his wetsuit on the railing. I watch him.

Little by little he re-emerges, becomes agreeable to me again. Wait till you hear this, he says. Wait till you hear this story! His eyes are large and open, nothing hidden. His hair curly and untamed. His white cotton T-shirt sticks to him, his thongs are flecked with sand. His hands are large and firm, although his voice is unsure, with a note of expectancy.

Tom puts the mug onto a coaster and sits at the foot of the bed and looks at me. 'Well, I've got something for you. Wait till you hear this.' He takes a sip from his drink. I get up and turn the radio off, then get back into the bed.

'It's an amazing story,' he says. 'It could be an idea for you, you know, something you might use.' He laughs and moistens his lips. 'The first thing was, I got up when it was light enough, at first light, and thought, I wonder what the swells doing. I'll walk down to Tamarama and have a look. It was up enough so I thought, I won't walk over to Bronte to check the swell out there, I'll walk back up the stairs, get into my wetsuit and risk it, just go in, because I wanted to go in.'

I make an approving noise and nod encouragement.

'So I came back and got into my wetsuit and walked all the way back down and headed over to Bronte,' he continues. 'Sorry – I forgot a part there – there's a bit of a side story. As I was going back up the stairs, there was a bloke, surfer fella, went down with a blue Aloha surf board. Now remember that bit, Sof. Oh yeah, I thought. I wonder where he's going. So I got into my wetsuit and locked the car and off I went down to Bronte. As I was walking along with my surfboard, this bloke with a goatee drove past and gave me a bit of a look. He looked at me and I looked at him wondering, what's he looking at?'

Tom picks up his mug and looks at me. 'Remember that, Sofia,' he says. 'That bloke. That's two fellas I've seen this morning.'

He laughs at what he can see is my impatience. 'Getting closer, Sof. I'm getting closer. Then I ran. I was really stoked. Good waves, the swell was pretty good. It was much better this morning than it looked last night. So I ran down to the southern end of the beach because there's a bit of a channel there near the rocks and you can have a go. A bit easier to get in. And I was sitting there on the sand. I was pretty tired. I'd run up those stairs and back down to the beach. So I'm doing a few stretches and then a lady came up. Starts talking to me. Said, Oh yeah, the waves look all right this morning and said, Oh yeah, and Okay, and then, Have a good day. She had a bit of a chat and then she walked off. So then I was just about to walk in. No. No. Hang on. I was standing up doing some stretches and I looked out and the bloke was out there by himself. The one with the blue board. He'd come in. And then he's yelling out to me. Hey! Hey! Mate, mate! And so I thought, what's going on here? What's going on? He was the only one out there and I was going to be the second one. So I go over and that's when this other bloke that I'd seen in the car appears on the beach. He was standing there too, about to go in.'

'It's incest,' a friend said, unable to disguise the sound of disgust in her voice. She was stirring a teaspoon of sugar into her latte as the day closed down. 'Except he's not related to you,' she added.

'It's a shame Tom is just that fraction younger than my eldest son,' I said. 'Only two weeks younger, but still.'

'So this guy with the blue board came over,' continues Tom, 'and says, Mate, there's a big shark out there and look at the size of the bite mark on my board. A bite mark on the board. I'd say it was that big,' he says with wide hands. 'The shark bit the whole nose off his board. He said he'd pushed the board into the shark. The other bloke who'd looked at me in his car said, What will we do? I don't think we'll go in here,

I said. And then one of the clubby guys came down and said, Oh –
because all three of us were standing there looking at this guy show us
his board. I said to him, Could you get the rubber ducky out and scare
the shark off for us? He said, Oh no. I can't do that. And I wouldn't
recommend you go out there. And then he said, Well, enter at your
own risk. So then Justin, the bloke in the car with the goatee said,
Come on. Let's go in. We're umming and aahing. He said, I might go
in close, and I said, I don't think so. Because it's pretty deep in close.
So then, this bloke took off, the bloke with the blue board and showed
everyone on the beach. So is that a good story for you, darling? Did I
tell it well? Did I?'

'Yes, Tom.'

'You sent me out as shark bait!'

I smile and lean back on the pillows and pull the sheet up under
my chin.

I said to Tom, I want you to stop spending money on me. Stop buying
me things. I don't like it. He looked at me in surprise, asked, If that's
what you want, I won't do it. I listen to what you tell me. Is that what
you want? I said it was. He started to suffer here in this room, for the
first time. He said he'd go home now if that's what I wanted. I let him
say it.

I hadn't seen J for twenty years when I'd bumped into him again that
first time. I'd always maintained a certain distance from the others at
the places where I'd worked. I liked them, I lunched with them, but
I didn't get involved. We'd travelled Australia as part of the same film
crew but I hadn't taken much notice of him then. He was so young.

So I was on the escalator moving downwards towards the train and
he was on the up escalator.

He called out at me as we passed – me going up, him going down.
He called out my name. 'Wait for me at the bottom,' he said. 'I'll come
down.'

He came down with his mountain bike balancing in one hand and a takeaway cappuccino in the other. He was still a very good-looking man although his face was rounder, more filled out, and there were streaks of grey at the side of his very black thick hair. When he kissed me on the cheek, I could smell what I thought was the exertion from the cycling. His dark unshaved face grazed my face.

'Hold this,' he said handing me his cup of coffee, 'and I'll write down your phone number. Let's get together. Soon. Next week.'

It's on a family holiday at the beach. We're together, Father and us, his children. I'm five years old. My father is in the middle of the picture. I recognise the big grin on his face, the way he's smiling, the way he waits for the moment to be over; his fixed grin, a certain tidiness to his dress, his impenetrable expression. I can tell it's hot, that he's weary, that he's anxious.

It's sunrise over the water through the palm trees. The empty beach. Living by the sea, watching and waiting. Trying to find a way to connect the pieces.

I met my new lover Tom at a party I'd gone to alone, and then he danced with me, held me closer, asked where I lived. I don't often go to parties. I wish I could remember what we did that first day. I remember sending him down the steps to look at the swell when he first woke up.

'Have you got a pair of thongs I can wear?' he said.

We laughed when I showed him mine that would barely cover half his foot.

You settle into a comforting routine. Just the two of you. Get up early and look out at the swell. You show your granddaughter, four-year-old May Ling, his photo.

'I'm not saying I don't like him,' she says. 'But I don't like his hair.'

'What's wrong with his hair?'

'It's curly.' She frowns.

'But I thought you liked curly hair. You told me I'm lucky because I've got curly hair.'

'But not curly hair on a boy!'

I was surprised that J recognised me. I was surprised by several things: his enthusiasm to see me, that he seemed so keen to meet up, and I was also surprised and impressed when he said that he was working as an executive producer on a television series – but later this turned out not to be true.

We stood there in the midst of people hurrying down the escalator who ran across the platform and jumped on the train. I could tell from the indicator that the train did not leave for another two minutes.

I did not think about him after I got on the train, maybe because he was so young and because I still had hopes for a relationship with another man I was dancing with at the time.

The tables are occupied outside the café at Bronte; the blue and white awning is down. There's a spare seat on the lounge just inside the front door and I cross to it. The parking policewoman is kept busy checking the parking meters and writing tickets. The other regulars are here, the ones who come at this time of the day. The woman with the baby. And there's the little white dog she ties up to the postbox outside. It's like sitting in a giant lounge room at this place. The waitress takes the baby outside to play with the buttons of the public phone. People get up from their seats and stand on the pavement watching for the white spouts of water. Whales out to sea today.

Meanwhile, the sky has turned into a light translucent grey above the pink glow of the setting sun. The sea is darker out towards the east. Four spike-headed palm trees stand at attention, their trunks encircled in knots.

J had complained about the harshness of the light in the lounge room, said that I needed to plan my lighting better. If I trusted him to do it, he would pull out the ceiling and put in a new lighting system. But I didn't trust him. Another time, he leaned over the balcony and said I should put some spotlights on to the rock formations leading to the gulley. All this he said he would do for me if I trusted him to do it.

In the school holidays, I took my granddaughter May Ling to my niece's house to play with her two children. Over a cup of tea, I asked my niece for memories of her grandfather, my father. I told her I'd spoken to the Aunt Gertrude in the Monteforie Home and that I wanted to find out more about our family history before everyone died.

'A lot of them are dead already,' she said. 'I only know they were Russian.'

'Russia and Poland. Your great-grandmother was Polish. She was Ben-Gurion's cousin, first cousin.'

'That's really something!'

My niece told me she remembered him being sick most of the time. 'Once I got to an age that I could remember things, I remember him as being sick, but he was quite a large presence really and I remember him in the big chair and he'd have trouble getting up and I'd often help pull him up. I really don't have memories of him, though. I remember the night he died and his funeral. It was at night. I was in bed and got up and realised that Mum and Dad were in the "grown-up" lounge room and Dad went to the hospital and they'd actually said "that was it" because he'd been in hospital for a while and I went back to my room and closed the door. I had photos of all my school friends on the back of the door and they all fell off. It was the spookiest thing. I didn't slam the door or anything. I remember the sound of the photos fluttering to the floor.'

The clouds stretch across the sky and move south. Tom rubs my shoulder a little. It doesn't really matter so much, does it, darling? Sometimes he massages my feet and I keep on reading. This time, I pull my feet out of his hands. He looks out at the dark blue afternoon sweltering on the sea, and sighs heavily and says he feels dreadful for upsetting me.

You have Sunday breakfasts. At the table next to you, three young men talk about Rugby while eating poached eggs on toast. This cove at Clovelly is protected from the ocean swells by the rocks. Iridescent green underside of flippers, bare-chested swimmers. Pigeons watch from the cement. Snorkellers looking for sightings of blue gropers and cuttlefish among the wildlife in this eastern beach. The occasional Port Jackson shark.

A plane flies through the low-hanging cloud over the cliffs. A woman by the rocks on a stone bench pats the shoulder of the man beside her in a friendly loving manner. The man's head, with its peaked white hat, scans the horizon.

The waves brush and break over the rocks that almost enclose the cove. Boys in flippers, snorkels and short wetsuits, with heads down, look for the family of gropers. Another man ducks his head down into the sea, fills his goggles with water, then empties them. With his head down, he floats towards the steps.

'There's no need to be self-conscious,' Tom says in the early morning light. 'There's no need to be. It's the person inside that's important.'

Through the open door, the same cool wind is breaking up the sea into chunks of moving white caps over there towards the horizon. Beside an upright and steady television aerial, down there near the beach, a palm tree sways in the breeze.

You find a photograph of your daughter when she was thirty. She's on the balcony with her own daughter. She's wearing a pale pink T-shirt and pearl earrings and her skin looks smooth and brown. Her smile is happy and bright. That's not how she sees herself, though, that attitude of someone happy in the moment.

He asks you questions about your family. 'What about your father?' he says. 'What did he do? What was he like?'

'My father was not an educated man,' you say, 'although he was well read. He was the eldest in a working-class family and he left school at the age of eight. He was a self-made businessman.'

'I remember him as being very pale,' my niece continued, before deciding we needed more tea. 'Very white hands. The translucent nails. Can't say I knew much about his personality. Only his physicality. It's very sad. Awful.'

Tom has strong muscled legs and large biceps. His arms grip so hard you have trouble releasing them and you can feel how tired they must get from all the paddling. He is very proud of his ability in the water and is ready for any emergency between the waves. Several times a week, he practises his manoeuvres, conditions permitting.

'You have fun with me, don't you?' he says.

'Yes.'

'We'll get through it. Don't worry. Everything will be okay.'

When your brother rings to see how you are, you say, 'I had a good weekend with Tom.'

'You mean your little surfie handbag!' he exclaims.

'Make sure he doesn't get your money,' your much older half-sister warns.

'What's his name again?' your eldest son says. 'I keep forgetting his name.'

'What do you expect me to say?' says your daughter. 'What do you want me to say?'

On the radio, 'It's really a beautiful day. I think God's out there having a swim.'

'What did your parents say?' you ask your new lover Tom.

'Dad said, Go for it, son. Mum said, Toy boy.'

'We used to go to visit every weekend,' my niece continued. 'On, I think, a Sunday afternoon. We'd go and visit them and he had his bedroom and he had an organ in there. And he turned the organ on for us while the grown-ups chatted. And I remember his bed, his space, the smells of his room. Not a nasty smell. You know, there was the smell of the books. It wasn't a weak smell. It was quite hard, really. A sharp smell. A sharpish smell. Not a horrible smell. Not a bad smell. I remember his pillbox next to the bed. It's the first time I'd seen one of those pillboxes that had the times of the day on it. And his little boxy room. And Nana had the gorgeous gilt bedroom, you know, and this huge bed and it was like Arcadia to a little girl. And then he had a single bed. I couldn't imagine such a large man in that bed. Papa's room.' She stumbled on the word, the name she used to call him, barely able to remember. 'I can't remember us playing in Nana's room,' she added.

Last night at the Sushi Train at Bondi Junction, a friend said, 'I chatted to a man while waiting in the queue at MBF this morning. An older German man. He was so interesting. I found his stories of Germany fascinating. There are stories everywhere,' she added, with a rising inflection in her voice and an arching of her eyebrows.

But how to tell them?

She mixed soy sauce into the wasabi paste. 'So you don't think you could love someone your own age?'

'Love someone at any age.'

'You don't love him?'

'The other day he said to me, You're well-educated and intelligent. Sometimes I wonder what you see in me.'

'What did you say?'

'I said what he wanted to hear. I said, You're so handsome and such a good lover. I didn't talk about my ambivalence.'

And the funeral? I said, reminding my niece that I was in South America when he died.

'Such a big step in the recovery process is the funeral,' she consoled me. 'We lived in Bulkara Road and that steep driveway and there were stairs and everyone used to just go up and down the driveway instead of using the stairs. Nana was standing at the bottom of the stairs saying, "I can't go. I can't go. I'm not going." Of course she went,' she added softly.

'And I wore…odd shoes! Which I didn't discover until later. Mum decided we were too young to go to the crematorium, so we went to the funeral – which I have no memory of now – I can't remember where it was – funny. I remember going in the car and then Mum sent us home with a friend of hers. When we got to the friend's house, she gave us lunch and I realised my shoes didn't match. My sister and I had two similar pairs of white shoes with little heels on them and I'd grabbed one of her shoes.'

'I heard he died trying to pull all the tubes out.'

'I didn't know he had an operation. The children weren't told. I remember the hospital, going there, walking through the courtyard. I don't remember being in a room with him. Sick! Isn't that funny?'

'He asked me if he'd been a good father and if he'd married the wrong woman.'

'That's why I think that I remember Nana saying, I don't want to go to the funeral, it's too upsetting. I always thought they were at war. I remember thinking, but he didn't like you.' She paused and looked at me, put her hand on mine. 'Life's not that simple, though.'

'Is there anything else you can remember?'

'I remember him being proud that I was smart,' she said, laughing at herself. 'I remember it being a big thing for him. Which is sort of an old European thing.'

Tom's skin is amazingly soft. A thin body, but strong in muscle tone. He's almost hairless. Perhaps he's weak, possibly too malleable, definitely vulnerable. I looked him in the face. Looked into his eyes. He touched me. Touched the softest parts of me, caressed me.

He is reluctant to mix with the people I know. He is just a boat builder, after all, and they may not take him seriously. Also, they might laugh at the way he speaks. They might laugh because this is the eastern suburbs of Sydney.

He does not consider himself to be intelligent, witty or articulate.

I breathe in the salt air and remember the taste of warm salt water on Tom's skin. I pause to watch as another wave rears up from the deep. A lone surfer out on the point. As I walk, the surfer drops down the face of a big left-hander. He paddles into the path of the wave. Another wave and he's kicking hard to mount it, rises to his feet before leaning into his first turn.

'An around the house cutback is when you go out on to the face of the wave away from the pocket and turn back in to the whitewash and then rebound off the whitewash and back around,' Tom says. 'You're really doing a cutback into a backhand re-entry off the foam. Two manoeuvres in one. It's a good point-scoring manoeuvre, the one I use the most.'

'Ask May Ling if she wants to come down for milk and cookies,' my niece called out to her son.

'And I have a memory of him at the Shabbat table and us crowding around him,' she said. 'But I think that memory comes from a photo, not from the real thing. How old was I when he died? He was very sick at my bat mitzvah. I would have been thirteen. He came out of hospital for my bat mitzvah and he came up to the bimah and I said, Can I put my arms around you? And I caught that he was wearing some sort of support thing under his shirt, I don't know what it was, and then I started to cry uncontrollably and everyone thought I was crying because it was my bat mitzvah, but I was crying because I felt that Papa was not right. And then he went back to the hospital and he didn't come to the party. He'd made a huge effort to come to the *shul.* You don't remember, you don't think about things at that age. I'd forgotten that memory and it came up. I remember thinking he was in a lot of pain and he struggled to be there.'

'What do you do when you're not working?' I ask Tom.

'You've asked me that before,' he says. 'Not a great deal.'

'I remember going to Nana's house and the photos of her from before, and I thought she looked just so glamorous. And going to Dad's factory and he was working with Papa and they had a wall of stuff they'd brought back from other countries – he'd gone to Japan and brought things back, and thinking he was Superman. Flying to other countries. But of course I've inherited Dad's view of the world so I know that Dad, "the genius", went into the family business and worked for his father for years and never really wanted to. Life was not what Dad wanted it to be – or he was unable to accept what his life was, put it that way. I remember now, at the *minion* at Nana's house, Dad…I think he'd probably been drinking…he was very emotional. He said if he hadn't sold the business that his father would never had died and that he had all these regrets and on the one hand he wished he'd never been in the business and then on the other hand he wished he'd held on to the business. I think a doctor told Dad that Papa had nothing to live for because the business had gone.'

'I heard him say that in hospital. I said to him there are so many things you can do now.'

My niece laughed bitterly, then said wistfully, 'Yeah. All those grandchildren. I'm so proud of my children. Lovely family. That's what's important.'

'Look at that,' says the waiter looking out at the sea. 'It's coming from the east. You can never pick it this time of the year, can you?'

He taps me on the arms, 'Are you parked down the road?'

'No. I'm on foot.'

I blow on the surface of the coffee, but it is still too hot.

A former heroin addict is being interviewed on the radio. 'I was solemn, angry and unhappy,' he says. 'Determined to destroy myself. The heroin alleviated doubt, unease, discomfort.'

'What was it like afterwards?' asks the interviewer.

'You feel very empty afterwards. I bottomed out. You have to decide, do you want to live or do you want to die? It was a deep character flaw with me.'

On the radio, 'Dangerous surf conditions with the time at five past nine.'

2

The Interview

'The interview is a position of teasing out information,' the woman with a PhD says from the leather chair under the photos of the famous writers. 'You're pushing and pushing trying to get something out.'

Kate is stretched out along the couch in the playroom in only underpants and a halter-neck top. It's very rare for my daughter and me to be spending time alone together now that she has the demands of a husband and two young children.

Above us, the ceiling fan is doing its best in the searing heat but the humidity is up near the hundred mark. Kate has the same faded blue eyes as me but her hair is the colour of cornstalks. We've been talking about the book she's reading and how the name of the author of the book is the same name as the character in the book, but the book is presented as a fiction.

'Put your hair up, take your shoes off,' Kate says. 'Everything helps.' She stands up and walks towards her bedroom.

Through the window, the gum tree casts an afternoon shadow on to the grass.

Kate returns with a short cotton skirt that used to be mine, then sits back down. 'You're not going to write about me, are you?' she says.

'No, I'm just needing to interview someone. It's part of the course.'

The baby calls out from the front bedroom.

'She's awake,' I say, unable to disguise the disappointment in my voice. 'Ruby's awake and now I won't be able to interview you.'

'Don't worry,' Kate says. 'Bring Ruby in and she can sit on my lap.'

In the bedroom, I lean over the cot and carefully pick up the baby. Her little red and white striped shorts cover the tender rolls of fat on her thighs. I kiss her soft cheeks, change her nappy, and bring her out to the back room. Kate feeds her raisins and I ask the question again. Her most important place?

'Here,' Kate says without hesitation. 'Here. This house. This house that we're trying to sell,' she sighs. 'This is my home. It is where my family is and my comfortable bed, where I am completely free to be me. I can make it as messy as I like or as neat as I want. I can help myself to the food and know exactly what's going to be here. Where I can lounge round in my comfies.'

'Comfies?'

'Daggy clothes or slippers. Comfortable clothes, braless and... trackies or sarong or my nightie.'

'Without the constraints of uncomfortable clothing?'

Kate nods and looks at her watch. 'We'd better get going. It's almost time to pick Conrad up from kindy.' She grins. 'You'll have to ask your new friend the question now.'

We pull our trousers back on and search around for our shoes before heading out the back door.

Still no sign of rain. Later on, the country gripped with drought, my nightmare is that I am lying on the floor all curled up trying to sleep on a hard surface with my back wedged up against a tall cupboard. The cupboard is full, and on top of it and behind it are heavy paintings and other bits and pieces that are weighing it down. The weight of all these things is causing the cupboard to become unbalanced. I can hear it strain as it stretches and creaks and then finally it topples over on top of me. I'm wedged in its axis. No injuries as far as I can tell, but there's no room for me to move at all. In a weak voice, I call out for help. But there is no one to hear.

'It's a miracle you got a job,' I said.

J's face changed, his eyes sad.

'I meant that you have a job that uses your skills and knowledge from the past,' I clarified. 'That there's a connection with your first love – photography.'

'You're back-pedalling,' he accused me.

I looked out across the window box of the restaurant to the grey road, remembering waiting outside the shop where he worked. I'd waited in the dark by the side of the road for him to come out and watched his workmates leave the premises. He didn't give the impression he wanted to introduce me to the people he worked with. He seemed happy enough to see me, though. Said something about how reliable I am. Said he felt safe with me.

I'd shown my daughter a photo of my new friend Tom, and the bracelet he'd given me the previous weekend, but she'd dismissed the bracelet with a glance and an 'Mmm' and the photo with 'Nice'.

I find a writing pad and pen and pick up the phone. By now, Tom will have finished helping his mother with the dishes and they'll be sitting on the couch in the lounge room watching Temptation on television. His father will probably be in the study playing around on his computer.

'Hello. Is Tom there?'

'Sofia,' says Tom's father. 'What's it like in your part of the world tonight?'

'A bit muggy and overcast. What about you?'

'Stormy,' he laughs. 'Things are pretty stormy here,' he continues, as if he expects me to understand the joke. 'I'll get Tom.'

Tom is living back home with his parents since splitting up with his wife two years ago. He said that his boys enjoy coming to stay with him every second weekend to see their grandparents. He alternates these weekends with staying at my place. 'My mum likes to have a chat,' he explained defensively. 'She likes having me here.'

'I think my dad likes you,' Tom says.

'Does he? What's your father's name? I don't know what to call him when he answers the phone.'

'Julian.'

'Tom, you know how I said I might want to interview you because I'm learning how to do interviews?'

'I remember. I remember you saying that. I remember everything you say,' he says proudly.

'So I want to ask you, where is the most important place to you?'

'A certain unit in Tamarama.' Tom laughs. 'The place where you live.'

'No, somewhere else. Like Avoca. The place where you live.'

'Avoca? Well, to be honest, I prefer Copacabana.'

Out the window, the branches of the pine tree move gently up and down and side to side in the sea breeze as I watch. And then, out of nowhere, it begins to rain.

'Have you got a cold?' I ask, noticing a thickness in his voice.

'Does my voice sound different? It's because I've been drinking. I've had a few beers with my mate who lives next door. We went down to the beach after work and had a few drinks.'

'I hope you can still answer my questions then?' I say, noticing my own tone of accusation.

'It's all right. I'm not an alcoholic. Just four beers. When I came home today, Mum said, "You smell of beer."'

I try to remember the beaches of the Central Coast he'd shown me that weekend when I'd caught the train to Gosford. I'd suggested he do the booking of the room for the two of us. 'Am I meant to pay for it all?' he'd asked in a whiny voice.

'So what do you want to ask me?' Tom says.

'What is the most important place to you?'

'Do you mean a beach or a house?'

'Whatever.'

'Do you mean in Australia or in the whole world? My favourite place in the world would have to be Medewi in Bali because it's got the longest left-hand break in the country. Twenty-seven years of surfing came together for me on one wave on that trip to Medewi. All those years of surfing came together – all the manoeuvres. That's what blew me away. It totally blew my mind. It's the best place for a left-hand wave.'

'A left-hand wave?'

'When you're standing looking at the surf to the left is a left-hand break. I'm a goofy footer with my right foot forward and I face the wave. A natural footer would face the surf on a right-hand wave with their left foot forward. When I came in from the surf that first day, I had caught so many waves. I'd made a bit of a pig of myself because I hadn't surfed such perfect waves in my whole life.'

I can hear the excitement in his voice down the telephone line. 'I'm writing down everything you're telling me,' I say. 'That's why I'm not saying much.'

'Have I told you what you want to know? Is it what you wanted?' he says with that contagious enthusiasm of his.

'Yes, I hope so. I have to type it up now.'

'On the computer? Are you typing as I'm talking?'

'No. I hope I can make some sense out of it all.'

'Have I made sense?'

'Yes, you have, but I don't know if I can make sense of it.'

'No one's ever asked me questions like that before. I'll tell Dad. I'll tell my dad I've just done my first interview. I've been interviewed. The champion surfer!'

The sea darkens and the thudding music starts up again in the house in front as I stand on the balcony looking out into the blackness. It's my fault that I didn't say anything. Right from the beginning, he had said that he might not be what I was looking for. I didn't know it would all feel like such a burden, just like with J.

I know the relationship with Tom will be short-lived. But I am at a crossroads: I know I need to make changes; I have no respect for a person who is unable to change. But everything I've done since the children left home has been a way of waiting for the next phase of my life to arrive. The problem is that when I try to imagine a future for myself all I can see is a black emptiness.

I cross back to the door and quickly return to the room.

At the front door, I don't pause but go through it and descend the stairs, which are in darkness, and then continue along a long hall, at the end of which is a sliver of light from the car park.

I wait in the foyer, which looks out on a garden made up of trees and shrubs that surround a courtyard. An elderly woman walks towards me. I stand up to meet the woman as she enters. The woman is wearing a blue and white blouse tucked into black trousers and flat black shoes. There is a youthfulness about her style of dress, or is it the speed with which she walks?

'I was out helping the gardener,' the woman explains.

Aunt Enid checks the buttons on her blue and white blouse as we sit down for lunch in the dining room at the home. She says, 'Anyone who complains about the food here doesn't know what they're talking about.'

'When the older ones die, it's lost forever,' she'd said on the telephone when I'd rung.

'Leba Samer and Elias Green, the real name was Greenbaume,' she says now. She's got the dates written on a piece of paper. 'They lived in Plontsk and left there to come to Australia in 1885. Ina was the eldest child. She was born in Plontz. Their eldest son was born in Australia in 1892.'

'Why did they leave Plontk?' I ask.

'Not a good place to live. They wanted a better life. Juda Green was the eldest boy, born in Australia in 1896.'

As the afternoon progresses, I begin to think she has nothing to tell me about Father.

'He was much older than us,' she apologises.

'I heard that he was given away as a child.'

'I don't know anything about that. He lived with us for a time at Leeton but he wasn't a child. A teenager or in his twenties.'

'What do you remember of him then?'

'He played in the football team.'

'When he was a teenager?'

'Or in his twenties. I really don't know,' she sighs with disappointment. 'I don't know much about him. He was much older. Much older. A front rower. In the scrum. Something like that.'

'How do you remember him as a person?'

'I think he was a very hard worker. Very proud of his children. Intellectually, I think he had a great brain. He could talk on a whole range of subjects. Politics or whatever. Sid held him in very high regard.' She nods, shakes her head. 'He was very proud of you kids. You know that, don't you?'

Tears well up but I don't reply, say instead, 'Were they related to Ben-Gurion? Was it true or was it a story?'

'Supposedly. I'm not sure. You know it was claimed. Grandpa Green was supposedly a cousin of Ben-Gurion.'

It's when we walk towards the front gate to say our goodbyes that I remember the question that I'm meant to ask before concluding an interview. 'Is there anything else you'd like to say?'

'I miss your mother very much,' she says. Then she kisses me goodbye.

The crashing of glass into bins. There is another crash, another amber glow from the horizon and the Norfolk Island pines glow in the dawn light. Two barefoot surfers, boards under their arms, jog in the exact same rhythm across the grass towards the beach. A tractor churns up the sand.

Tom rubs the Cancer Council Factor 30 cream into his face as I watch. I am lying in the shade under a Norfolk Island pine and he knows I am watching him carefully.

'At home, I'm surfing with world champions,' he says. 'Here, I get as many waves as I want – they're all beginners.' He grins. 'I thought you would have got rid of me ages ago. I've never had a long-distance girlfriend before. We've come a long way since that first night.' He motions for me to help zip his wetsuit up at the back.

'You're the nicest chick I've ever been out with,' he says. 'I've told you that before. These are the best weekends when I come down to see you. Am I what you wanted when you went looking? Have I come up to scratch?'

Silent clouds in the pale sky.

The next morning, J and I had walked along the beach and then along the cliffs towards Coogee. He stopped for a cigarette and we sat on a rock looking out to sea. The slap of waves against rocks below us. Board riders sank into the swollen water of rips. When we got to Coogee, he wanted to catch a taxi back to my place.

I laughed. 'No wonder you have no money. You spend it on taxis and expensive bottles of wine.'

He had another cigarette and rested before we walked back along the coast.

'You must be exhausted,' I say to Dr Ross. 'Seeing all these people and hearing all their problems one after the other.'

'Some psychiatrists are very precious about that,' he says.

'What do you mean?'

He shrugs. 'They make a big fuss, whereas…'

'You must feel the need to unload at the end of the day?' I say. 'To unburden yourself?'

He smiles. 'So how are things going with the surfer?'

'My friends tell me he seems very devoted to me.'

'He's reliable, generous with his time, prepared to drop his trousers whenever you want. A lot of people would be very envious.'

With his left hand, the doctor caresses his tie before adding, 'He makes no emotional demands on you. You could stop punishing yourself about it. Tom's a grown-up. You're not responsible for him. He'll go if he's not happy. If he wants out, he'll end it.'

My three-year-old grandson and I kick a soccer ball around in the backyard. Afterwards, we colour in at the kitchen table. When we've finished the stories before bed and I'm lying with him on the bed breathing in the smell of his hair, I ask him what he wants to be when he grows up.

'A helicopter,' he says without hesitation. 'I want to be a helicopter.'

I laugh as we lie back looking up at the stars that his mother, my daughter, has painted on his ceiling.

'You can show Tom my collection of DVDs,' he volunteers. 'And when you're all grown up and have your own kids, you can borrow one of my DVDs and take it home.'

My daughter listens from the hallway. She hurries into the room and says to her son, 'Grandma is grown up already. She's had children already. Do you know who her children are?'

He thinks about her question. 'No.'

'Who is mummy's mummy?'

'Grandma.'

She nods. 'That's right,' she says. 'She's old. Grandma is old.'

'Don't say that to him,' I say.

She shrugs. 'Sorry.'

Aunts…how I have used them. Their memories supply the many-coloured threads that I need to see the patterns. They lead me into their dark cramped rooms with a single bed, a table by the window – photos, letters, treasured cross-stitch pictures on the walls – their voices hushed over tea and sandwiches, distracting me from my quest with their bony hands that cradle porcelain cups, the folded lines on their fingers like the ribboned feet of seagulls. The tops of their hands are stained with what look like splashes of mud, their crooked fingers displaying silver and gold and diamonds as their hands rest on the tablecloth through loose white cotton or bright polyester sleeves.

My father's story is not a well rounded story. At best, I have been able to encapsulate brief moments, as in a dream. There are only the moments I have mentioned already, nothing else. I have found no comfort in these glimpses, no real understanding.

On the telephone, Aunt Cynthia says, 'Inez and I didn't know your mother had converted to Judaism until she died. She didn't tell us. What a funny strange hurtful background we come from. None of us had it easy as children. You didn't either. She favoured your brother. I've thought about it and wondered why she treated you like that. I think it was because she wasn't ready when you were born. You turned up too soon after he was born. There's only thirteen months between you, isn't there? You came too soon. She wasn't ready. That wouldn't happen these days. I could see you felt unloved when I came to stay at your place when my own children were born. I could see what you meant. You said something to me when I was staying there. I can't remember your exact words. You must have been ten, I'll think about it, but I can remember being there in your house and I could see what you were talking about.

'My mother, your grandmother, never got over the death of Margaret from cerebral palsy. Who wouldn't want to throw themselves off the Gap, if you think about it? Her first child born with cerebral palsy – her little girl sick for six years and then dead. And stuck in that flat in Edgecliff. Her son sent off to Queensland because there wasn't enough money and then he's killed in the war. You wouldn't have to be nutty to want to jump off the Gap after all that. I paid the money to have her grave cleaned up. Your mother should have been doing that.

'I told you before, Inez was my mother's favourite and I was your mother's favourite. My mother gave a lot of love to Inez. When Inez rang me last time, she was saying she really misses her mother and what a wonderful person she was and she wishes she'd tried harder when your mother was alive. But that's just not true. She was an awful person.

'The three of us slept in the two beds when Inez would come and visit. My father was very generous to have your mother living here and Inez when she'd come in the school holidays.'

'Inez said she didn't get to come home in the school holidays.'

'I know she says that but I don't remember it that way. I remember her being there. It was my room and I was put out by sharing it with the two of them. Inez's childhood is all coming down on her now that she's in her seventies. It wasn't easy for me either. I had them living in my room, your mother and Inez. Inez was a quiet little thing and my mother loved her. My mother gave Inez a lot of love. Inez would do all the jobs. Do the housework and she didn't cause any trouble.'

Dawn through slatted blinds. A ridge now visible and the dark green of the crepe myrtle. A soft cool light that lasts for only as long as I can hear the birds. In a few minutes, the morning haze will be replaced with searing heat, ablaze with building machinery next door and the sounds of traffic grinding up the hill.

Rivers of water down the glass. The rain pelts down on top of the car. Headlights through grey. The rain swooshes down the hill and echoes on the roof.

Tom's thick black steamer of a wetsuit and his beach towel hang over the railing of the balcony, the towel still damp after several hours in the morning warmth. Out to sea, the sun glistens on the arch of a wave and sends sparkles over the ocean.

'What were you saying just now about the southerlies in winter?' I ask him. 'I didn't know the waves were different in summer and winter. You said something about the southerlies?'

'In summer, the surf's onshore,' he says. 'The nor-easter onshore winds that are at most beaches. The surf's usually small in summer and crowded. Winter's much nicer because the surf's often bigger through the southerly winds – it picks the swell up. Less crowds, and you don't get bluebottles. You just have to brave the cold in a thick wetsuit.'

'Thick wetsuit?'

'A sealed seamed wetsuit so the water doesn't get in.'

'Sealed seamed? Aren't summer wetsuits sealed?'

'No. A lot of people just wear board shorts or spring suits.'

'Spring suits?'

'Spring suits are from here,' he says touching my thigh from behind. 'To here,' he says touching my forearm. 'I wear a spring suit all summer long,' he adds.

'For sun protection?'

'My sort of skin is like yours. I have to protect it.' He sighs into my ear. 'That's about it then,' he concludes.

I laugh and he laughs too.

On the radio a voice sings, 'It's a new dawn. It's a new day.' The radio announcer says, 'A beautiful day in Sydney. A beautiful blue sky, although it's going to be humid again.'

Tonight, there are three stars visible between the low-hanging cloud and the darkened sky. I breathe in the cool air – the sweet, slightly exotic scent of summer – then look up at the deep unknowable night. The clouds are full and bunched and draped with grey. Higher up, they expand and thicken, then disappear into black. And there's the ghost moon hanging to the east, enormous and simple in its circular arcs. I feel its warmth.

'I only rings you because there's no one else to ring,' a friend had reprimanded me. 'You'll never get your needs met with someone like him. He's very appealing. He'll get you in and then drag you down with him.'

Breathe in and exhale, instructs the yoga teacher. Stretching up. Tail bone under. Reach tall. Really breathe. Right leg back. Really stretch. Inhale and look up, exhale and back to plank. Straight up and into down dog. Reaching forward. Breathe in. Exhale. Curl your tail bone under. Hands shoulder width apart. Back to plank. Optional push up, breath in. Move your shoulders away from your ears. Walk, or lightly jump, forward. Breathing in, breathing out. Right leg back. Exhale right down to plank. Then back to downward dog. Breathing in, rolling up, reaching tall. Into chair pose. The option is to lift your heels, ankles together. And back to plank, and back to downward dog. Walking or jumping forwards, reaching upwards. Catch your breath. And exhale.'

The rain eases and turns into a brief shower so now there is only the gentle patter of water falling on the steel of the balcony railing. I open the sliding glass door and walk out and look up at the sky. The sweet smell of earth after rain.

3

Behind the Window

Perhaps loving something is the only starting place there is for making your life your own. – Alice Koller

A woman was feeding her six-week-old grandson from a bottle of breast milk. It was summer, and bright outside. On top of the Balinese cabinet that stood along the wall the sequinned headband of a golden reclining Buddha glinted in the sunlight. Inside the cabinet, the strains of an exotic tango strummed insistently from the radio as the light caught the mirrors of the embroidered cushions where she sat with her grandson. Their heads were inclined towards each other, eyes locked, fingers entwined, like two lovers.

The baby's hand was wrapped around her index finger and she had the middle finger of her other hand on that soft tender spot under his chin to remind him to keep sucking. The woman's jacaranda-blue eyes stood out beneath her long dark hair. She watched the bubbles of milk as she leant down and kissed the top of the baby's head and breathed in the sweet fragrance of his hair. In her arms, her pale-skinned, fair-headed grandson kept on sucking. For a moment, he broke away to catch his breath, releasing the teat and arching his back. The woman sat the baby up on her lap with one hand on his diaphragm and the other under his chin supporting his neck as his head flopped forward like a newborn puppy's. He burped.

The telephone rang. 'I'll only answer it if it's your mummy,' she said, letting the answer machine pick up the call. 'I don't want to speak to anyone. Not when you're here.'

But her words were drowned out by a loud swell of cicadas grinding and grating outside. She put a towelling nappy over her shoulder and walked with the baby across the parquet floor towards the sliding doors. She closed the doors gently. She paused, stared out through the glass across to the Pacific Ocean at Bondi, to the horizon and the sky, watched the waves glide across the sea as the wind blew from the south. She had waited a long time for this moment – had to wait for her daughter to be ready to hand over the baby so she could feed him the bottle – to have him to herself. It was one of the happiest moments of her life: just the two of them, in a tender embrace, her own golden-headed boy.

On the radio, 'That was Piazolla's tango. There are people whipping into church halls all over Sydney to dance the tango. They take off their grey cardigans, put a red flower behind their ears…'

I'd written that years ago and thought it made a good beginning for something. But my daughter had been upset when I showed it to her.

'He's not *your* golden-haired boy,' she said. 'He's mine.'

I get up from the desk where I have been working and look out at the sky. I've sensed a change in the weather. The leaves of the maple tree shake so vigorously in the wind it's like a frantic chiming of bells. The smell of rain is in the air as the golden leaves fall to the ground.

I can tell that I must be settling into this new place that I've moved to. This morning after I went outside to post some letters, I'd picked a frangipani from the tree next door and one pink hibiscus and a bunch of white sweet-smelling flowers and brought them in and put them in that small pink vase that used to belong to my daughter. The vase matches the pink hibiscus that softens the harsh black and the dark blue of the bathroom.

I turn and walk along the wooden corridor to the bedroom then cross the kitchen and out through the back door to the garage.

In the parking area at the club, I pause before deciding to park in one of the directors' spaces as I've done many times before. It's not as if a director of the RSL is likely to be at the club on a wet Tuesday night.

'Wet nights are a good time to come to tango,' a friend had said. 'A lot of women don't go out on wet nights.'

I walk in, say hello to Kevin at the desk. 'Do you want to see my membership card?'

'Yes,' he says from behind the reception area with a welcoming smile. 'It's been a long time since you were here last.'

I put the umbrella in the stand and enter the room.

As it's early evening, this part of the club is still well lit, although the wooden dance floor is separate from the general bar area. The poker machines are in an adjoining section. There's a proper platform now for the DJ to operate from and on which Carlos has placed his case of CDs. It's a big black zip bag with the disks displayed in plastic pouches. The lid of the grand piano next to the platform is up and the piano is ready for the three-piece tango trio who will perform twice during the evening.

Tonight, though, I have come for the lesson only and I don't intend to stay for the *milonga* or for the performance by the trio. It's taken all my willpower to get here for the lesson and that will do for the first time back to tango. I place my coat on the back of one of the chairs and look around for a friendly face.

'It's good for you to dance,' a married friend had counselled. 'Just treat it like a job. You just have to go there. That's what I'd do.'

'Yes,' I'd sighed. 'I wish I was as self-disciplined as you. To just be able to…to be able to do the things that I know are good for me.'

'What's the point in sitting at home? It's no answer.'

'There is no answer.'

The friend looked so self-satisfied in the sunlight with her pink mottled skin, glasses, pretty, determined face. 'One night a week to begin with. Don't overdo it and don't expect too much. Just go for the dancing.'

'That's all I go for.'

'Don't get caught up in all the other stuff.'

I'd come home late and went to bed and lay there in the dark, nervous, thinking about J, wishing he were with me, then sleeping lightly for only a moment or two before waking again to think about him. I'd looked forward to seeing him each time and hoped I wouldn't be disappointed.

If the bedroom curtains were open, I saw every detail of him by moonlight, the outline of him against the dim sky outside, but at the same time I knew his face so well I could see that, too, and even what his expression was.

I talked very little about him during the time we were together, which is surprising considering he occupied my thoughts most of my waking life. I thought mostly of the irritations, my confusion, my obsession with him and my frustration that I wasn't able to concentrate on my work. So now that I'm trying to bring him to life in my mind, I'm relying on memory and my own ability to create him like a character in a novel. I can't remember really important things about him, like the way the light fell on to his face, or the touch of his skin.

Nothing had changed last night. The same insincere air-kissing on both cheeks, the same 'in crowd' at the top table, the same daggers across the room from the other women.

The new teacher said I have a lovely quality to my dancing.

I told him I've been dancing for twenty years: ballroom, Latin American, salsa, ceroc. 'But only two years of Argentine tango. I used to dance four or five nights a week.'

'I could tell there was something,' he said. 'Why don't you do it still?'

'I got sick of the whole scene. And tango is the worst.' I looked up into his kind eyes. 'Very cliquey.'

'I've heard people say that but I don't see it.'

'Not enough partners. It's the usual story.'

Seagulls, their backs to the westerly, float on the sea, chests puffed out like plastic bath ducks. Low-slung grey cloud. The clouds press down on me.

At the marina at Rose Bay, a cyclist, proud of his bulging crutch in his iridescent cycle trousers, taps his helmet down on the next table before going to the counter to order a coffee. He gets out a white plastic rain jacket from the back pouch of his bright blue cycle top before sitting down on that chair with the legs that keep dipping into the gap between the wooden planks of the pier.

A waiter brings a short black to the table. 'Where did you ride today?' the waiter asks the cyclist.

I can't hear the reply but I hear one of the shipwrights calling out from one of the cruisers moored on the marina. 'It's winter, mate,' he yells as a man and a woman enter the café.

The man looks up at the Australian flag flapping on a corner of the pier. 'The wind is coming this way.' He gesticulates to the woman. 'Sit here with your back to the door. You'll be out of the wind.'

I watch as the waves break on shore, so small from this angle that I can barely see them, only a flickering of white; stagnant oily bubbles on the surface of the harbour.

It looks like rain. The flags dance to the rhythm of the westerly as submerged weeds drift beneath the surface of the water. The café already in shadow. Time to go home.

I walk quickly up the hill passing a construction site on the way.

'Don't go under the ladder,' a workman calls out. 'You know what they say about ladders!'

'I've seen the sky look like this before,' Tom had said enveloping my waist with his arm.

'What do you mean?' I'd asked, and looked at him: his face was amazing, a unique arrangement of angular bones and taut skin, so innocent, with his country ways, not full of jaded city ironies, but a surfer's curved legs and muscular shoulders and a finely balanced frame.

'So still,' he said in that gentle dear voice. 'A winter sky.'

Watching the sky was one of the few things we had in common.

'You made an odd couple,' my daughter said in an effort to console me. 'You'll break his heart,' she'd warned when we got back together the first time.

Dark clouds float behind the water tower as I watch. There is a glimpse of bright white behind the hills at Dover Heights and a line of light behind the ridge as the tree in front continues to lose its leaves.

At one of the most difficult stages of my life, I feel that I've been rescued by a beautiful building. I can't believe my luck. Just six steps in through the door and I said, 'I'll take it.' The whole place is enormous, with magnificent rooms, high ceilings, lots of light and even water glimpses across to Rose Bay. I would have taken it sight unseen, it being art deco and on the top floor. It does look very old and neglected from the outside but that means the rent is reasonable. Six apartments in the block, two on each level.

I never planned to move back here, the place where I spent the first sixteen years of my life, but six months after moving in I can't imagine living anywhere else. Just up the hill from the harbour and just down the hill from the newsagent, the greengrocer, the post office, the florist.

The block of units straddles two streets on the side of a hill, the front door on one street and the back door on another. The main opportunities for residents to bump into one another are in the common laundry or when using the front door. My garage is level with the back door so I only use the front door when going for a walk or if I take one of the grandchildren to the park next door.

When I exit the building at the lower street, another resident might be playing with his dog on the lawn, or kicking a football with his son, or cooking sausages on a portable barbecue. The residents are very friendly so I don't want to put anyone offside by reporting the forbidden cats and the dog or for the mess they leave on the landings and in all the common areas: kids' bikes, balls, a plastic sandpit, a blackboard and trucks, an old pram in the drying room; the smell of cat urine on the stairs. But who cares?

The man in the unit next door said, 'I've got five new friends in this place. If I need anything or am in trouble, they'll be there for me.'

At first, I was wary of this man with his kitchen door open and the television blaring and the cigarette smoke and the empty bottles of bourbon and coke.

I said to the woman who lives on the top floor at my old place that I was very happy to get out from down in the dungeons of the bottom floor.

The woman pulled a face and said, 'Remember what happened to us? Now you'll have all the roof problems.'

The pest control service man calls on Monday: a dark-haired, middle-aged man wearing heavy boots. As soon as he enters the landing, having climbed four flights of stairs to get here, he leans back against the wall, panting. This will be the ninth possum he's collected from the roof of this block of units, he points out.

'It looks like a nice place where you live,' he says when he comes down the ladder from the roof with a possum in his cage.

Possum poo falls on to the red carpet as he puts the cage down on the landing.

'Come and have a look,' he invites me.

I go over to the cage and watch as he dangles his keys in the possum's face and the possum bares his teeth and hisses.

'He's a big one,' I say.

'Not that big. I'll give him another apple to eat on his way to the Botanic Gardens.'

'That's kind of you.'

'I try to imagine what the possum's thinking. He wouldn't have been in a car before.'

I'm waiting for the possum man to go so I can get back to work, but he keeps talking. I sense he may have another agenda. He tells me how much it costs the agent every time he, the possum man, comes to the block of units with one of his cages and the price of his petrol to get here and to take the possum to a far away park. He said it costs him a lot in money and time from his house in Liverpool.

'You must be paying a lot of rent,' he comments. 'How much do you pay?'

'A lot,' I say moving back towards the door.

He kicks the possum droppings towards the banister. After all, it's not part of his job to clean up the mess. It's the cleaner's job. He picks up the cage and walks towards the stairs.

Does he think I want to invite him in? Is that why he's hovering at the door? Or was it because I gave him my card? We exchanged cards last time when he left the cage in the roof.

'Just ring me any time,' he said.

I close the door and go back to my desk by the window.

J had accused me of falling in love with him. He said that's why he needed to end it the first time. 'I don't want to feel responsible if you fall in love with me,' he said. 'I've got enough problems looking after myself without worrying about someone else.'

After this conversation, he offered to walk me to my car.

'Don't bother,' I said.

'Should I ring you in a couple of weeks?' he called out.

'Whatever,' I shrugged.

The golden-haired boy turned five last week and gave me an invitation to his Batman party. When I arrived early at the party wearing my Batgirl outfit and to give my daughter a hand, Kate went into a spin and said she'd have to dress up too.

During the afternoon, a male friend told Kate that she looked great. Kate had tucked her pants into high boots, added a leather belt, long black gloves, drawn the shape of cat's eyes with a black kohl pencil.

'I had to do something,' Kate said to her friend. 'When my mother arrived dressed like that.'

The maple tree stands stiff and bare as the sky lightens and the rain begins to ease. Light streams in along the ridge as the dark clouds open.

Two darkly feathered willy wagtails stand like sentinels on the leafless branches. I watch the occasional twitch of their tails. It's like a spasm that needs to be scratched in order to relieve the itch.

When the afternoon light begins to fade, the sky thick and grey behind the green of the magnolia tree, my daughter looks out the window and says, 'Those magnolias are all brown.'

She sighs when she says it and I seem to recall that she touches her ear, perhaps turns the gold circular earring that I used to watch her do in that pensive way of hers. She's always loved magnolias. When they first moved into their new house, she said what a lovely surprise it was to discover that they had magnolias in the garden. If I were her, I'd be bringing magnolias into the house while they're still in bloom.

Last night, I read the golden boy two stories before he went to bed. It's my job to make sure he cleans his teeth and does a wee before the story. Since he was born, I have gone over every week to see my daughter and to give a hand. I stay on and cook dinner for the family before going home. It's a comforting routine and I get to see them regularly.

In the afternoon, we'd played paper aeroplanes and sent them flying from the top of the stairs. I blew bubbles and he chased them before slicing them in two with the sword of his Lego superhero. His little sister ran around too, trying to break the bubbles by swinging at them with the hair of her Brat dolly.

During the afternoon, my daughter seemed distant and irritable so I'd kept my distance. When I was leaving, she said, 'Maybe it's best if you don't come when I'm in a bad mood.'

I looked at her, puzzled.

'You always take it on board,' she accused me.

I drove home in silence. That night I lay awake, on edge, waiting for something to happen. How long could this go on?

Now down at the marina a seagull struts across the railing of the pier with proud red webbed feet. Patterns of water glide east and towards the shore on the beach. Dark sky as the clouds move quietly towards the west.

'I've painted that little beach,' an artist friend had said. 'I tell my art students, keep a journal of anything that moves in your daily life – as you travel to work, or wherever you are.'

The seagulls look out towards the horizon as a line of bright light is attempting to penetrate the white thick cloud. Their chests are all puffed up as they scan the vista ahead.

'I won't come if you don't want me there,' I said to Kate later.

'I thought you were the one in a bad mood,' she explained.

I sighed. 'We're enmeshed, you and me.'

'It's worked well for this long,' she reassured me. 'We just had one bad week.'

What I need is a new definition of luck, like sitting here at this café watching the colours of the sunset over the sea.

The waiter with the ponytail brings in the big canvas umbrella from the sidewalk now that dusk is approaching. 'A beautiful day today,' he says.

'I like to come down here at this time.'

'I like this time of the day best,' he agreed. 'Everything is slowing down.'

On Tuesday I bumped into my psychotherapist friend Miriam Glass: a fair-skinned, middle-aged woman, Jewish, who was walking her dog in Cooper Park. We haven't seen each other for a long time. We chatted away as the dog squatted on the grass.

'And how are things with Kate?' Miriam asked. 'Last time I saw you, they were having problems.'

'They're still having problems and unfortunately I'm the one she takes it out on.'

Miriam nodded with understanding before wrapping her hand in a plastic bag and picking up the dog poo. Miriam looked calm and wise: grey at the temples, freckles, sensitive eyes. 'That's because you're her mother,' she pointed out, 'and she knows she can do that and you'll still love her.'

I breathed in the crisp clean air. So nice to be out in the park after the rain. 'It's very hurtful,' I said.

'How did she go with the second baby?'

'The same thing happened. But it took her a long time to get help. No one wants to be on medication. I had to force her to make an appointment to see the doctor. She'd taken herself off it.'

'She turns in on herself.' Miriam sighed.

I nodded. 'That's right. She's not assertive with him. She's like me in that way.'

With the cold of night settling in, some facts become clear to me. It's as if I am at the edge of a flat murky body of water that stretches on and on. Looking out at the murky, huge, cold expanse of water, I know that I should have known better. I can see this. I came to see it when I was at rock bottom, when I'd given up all hope. Now, a shapeless dread works its way inside me.

I sit by the window as the morning sun rises above the ridge. Now that the maple tree has lost all its leaves I can see the whole of the ridge, especially that part at Dover Heights where the sun first appears. It's the first winter that I've lived in this place and the first time I've been able to see what is behind the leaves of the maple tree.

A bus changes gear with great effort as it makes its way up the hill. I watch two lorikeets sitting on a bare branch of the maple tree. A man hammers on steel. Are the birds entwined in battle or is it lovemaking as their necks lock urgently at the throat?

The lorikeets fly off and a willy wagtail lands on the top branch of the maple tree in front of the window.

I must learn to release my grip.

I feel the winter warmth on my face and on my weathered hands.

In the distance a bird calls out and another bird answers. I wait there at the window, in between the sounds.

I sit there day after day, relentlessly.

Possums are in the roof of the guest house in Bundanoon where I'm staying for the weekend. On the Friday when I arrived, I saw a man with a ladder and a cage about to climb up into the manhole. I asked him if he was the possum man.

'I'm the Everything man,' he replied. 'The gardener, the carpenter, the odd job man.' The Everything man smiled at me in a friendly manner and continued on his way up through the manhole. His long body eased itself up into the darkness and with him went his grey moustache, his tobacco smell and his friendly demeanour.

Today he's returned bearing a ladder, a torch and thick gloves on both hands. He apologises for the disturbance during the night, for the banging and crashing of the possum trying to get out of the cage.

'So that noise was an animal trapped in a cage?' I say, assuming the role of a character in a story. 'The noise went on from eleven o'clock until four this morning, when it must have collapsed with exhaustion.'

'Sorry about that,' he says before climbing up the ladder. 'We're trying to find where the possums keep getting in and out of the roof. Don't get too close,' he warns. 'When they come down from the roof, the possums are very frightened and wee everywhere. Stand back.'

He reappears through the manhole with a possum clinging to the bars of the cage. He tips the cage to the side. 'She's not very old,' he says.

'How do you know?'

'She's not very big.'

He gives the possum in the cage to his offsider, who will set her free in Moreton National Park. Then he stays there on the landing discussing the plight of the possum trapped in the roof. 'I just love possums,' the Everything man says. 'When I look into their eyes, I… just melt.' He pretends to fall to the floor. 'I felt claustrophobic up there myself. Just going up into the roof. I don't like being in a confined space.' He laughs to himself. 'I go caving, though. But that's a choice thing. I go into the cave as far as I can and then I come out again.'

Back in my room, I'm in a hurry to lace up the thickly grooved rubber-soled shoes. I wrap a scarf around my neck, stuff my gloves and woollen hat in the pocket of my waterproof jacket.

I want to get out there before the mist rolls in across the Southern Highlands.

Part Four

Four years later, by chance I saw J again. I needed to get a new passport photo taken and there he was in a dark blue uniform working in a photographic shop. He looked older.

'Thank you for everything you did to help me,' he said after an exchange of pleasantries.

'I helped you get a job,' I said modestly, although I knew I'd done plenty to help him.

'Yes, I needed a job,' he said. 'I needed the stability.'

What surprised me the most was when he said that he got married last year.

'What's her name?' I asked.

'Lucinda. She's a visual arts teacher.'

I couldn't hold myself back, so I asked, 'How long did you know her before you got married?'

'Two and a half years before the marriage. But I'd known her before. She knew what she was getting into. She's a friend of an old girlfriend of mine.'

'I'm very happy for you, J,' I said with sincerity in my tone. 'Things seemed to have worked out very well for you.'

'Up and down,' he said, spreading his arms out wide. 'Up here, and down there. Her mother died recently.'

When we said goodbye at the door of the shop, he said, 'We could have a coffee sometime?'

'Sure,' I said in my most light-hearted voice.

'Don't start up with him again,' advised my best friend Annalyse when I told her I'd seen him again. 'You're not going to do that, are you?'

I shrugged.

An environment of possibility. A black bird swings back and forth on the branch of a tree but then, like a bullet out of a gun, the bird is gone. Two kookaburras sit on guard on the television aerial on the house next door. They look this way and that arching their necks in their search for food. The morning sun turns their heads into flashes of bright white feathers.

Things do change, and as more time goes by, more things change.

'I bumped into J the other day and he's married now,' I tell my daughter while she's making me a cup of tea in her kitchen and I'm biting into a freshly baked Anzac cookie. She made the cookies while the golden-boy and his little sister sat up on the kitchen bench.

'Who was he again?' she asks as I look out the window to the power boats moored to the pier, their flags waving in the wind.

'He was the one before Tom.'

'That was quick. Or did he know her already?'

'It's been four years already. He knew her from before.'

'Did I meet J? I can't remember.'

'No. You never met him.'

A canvas-covered boat turns full circle in the breeze as I watch. Unexpectedly a small runabout jets out into the water. I hear the dull roar of its motor, and keep watching as a lone man, standing high at the controls, steers the boat toward the misty headland.